Planet Peace

Dr. Rosemary M. DePasque

Library of Congress Control Number: 2010908147
ISBN: Hardcover 978-1-4535-1553-2
Softcover 978-1-4535-1552-5
Ebook 978-1-4535-1554-9

This book was printed in the United States of America.

To order additional copies of this book, contact:
Xlibris Corporation
1-888-795-4274
www.Xlibris.com
Orders@Xlibris.com
80296

Contents

Dedication

This book is lovingly dedicated to my parents,
Rose D. DePasque and James B. DePasque,
with gratitude for all of their support,
encouragement, and humor.

Chapter 1

A Letter Found in a Time Capsule

Margo was walking her Jack Russell Terrier, Franklin, when she saw the large metallic box in the middle of a field. She lived in a hilly, rural area of eastern Pennsylvania, and people were starting to build some very strange-looking homes there. At first, when Margo and Franklin enjoyed these walks, they would occasionally see a beautiful, old, red barn amid the vast green hills. Trees, cows, sheep, and ponds also dotted the landscape. Recently, more and more people were building enormous homes of various styles in this area. It was heartbreaking for her, as she missed the simplicity of her agrarian town.

"I've heard of contemporary, but *this* is *ridiculous*!" she muttered to Franklin, as they walked by the structure. Something about it caught her eye, and she stopped abruptly. As Margo moved closer to the box, she could see handprints embedded in the metal, as well as cryptic writings all over the roughly twelve-square-foot cube.

Hello and welcome!
What you see,
Is a way for you to be
Truly free!

Please come closer,
You will find,
That this is not a figment
Of your mind!

What stands before you
Is not just a box,
With nuts and bolts,
And mysterious locks,

But a vehicle to
A distant land,
It all begins
With the touch of your hand!

These words were in the midst of various symbols and shapes. Margo speculated that the owner of this new home had quite an imagination! This couldn't be all that there was to it. Since the writings seemed to be on each wall of the cube, she assumed that this thing must be either a large lawn ornament, or the doorway to an underground home. She placed her hands on a set of handprints, but nothing happened. There were three sets of handprints on each side. Margo tried a few more sets of handprints, and then she began to feel silly. She looked around nervously, picked up Franklin's leash, and continued home.

When the construction crew arrived to excavate the land, they found a large metallic box right in the middle of the property. The foreman called the main office to confirm that the site was correct. The secretary informed him that it was indeed correct, and that the owners were on their way to take pictures of the excavation process. The men set about trying to lift and move the box. It would not budge.

The owners of the property pulled up in a vintage Lincoln Town Car. A man got out of the car. "Is this your idea of a joke, Joe?" he asked.

"I was going to ask you the same thing, Mr. Peterson," the foreman answered.

"So you're telling me that you have no idea where this contraption came from?" Peterson queried.

"Absolutely no idea, sir," Joe replied.

The crew of men read the poem and laughed. Some of them even placed their hands on some of the prints. There was nothing left to do but to try the backhoe. But all attempts to lift the box failed.

Later, Margo was driving by on her way to the grocery store when she saw the workers trying to move the box. She shook her head. She saw a well-dressed couple looking very frustrated, and a very determined group of men being unsuccessful. Then it occurred to her, "They don't want it there. Then who put it there?" She stopped the car. She couldn't stop herself from getting out and walking across the field. They barely noticed her coming up behind them. "Excuse me," she said, "I couldn't help but notice. Isn't the box yours?"

"No!" the couple replied in unison. "We were supposed to break ground today," the woman said.

"Oh, not having any luck, eh?" she offered.

"No!" they both replied.

After several minutes of watching the futile attempts to move the box, Margo said," It's interesting, isn't it? I happened to walk by this morning with my dog, and I was drawn to it by its mystifying symbolism. I thought it was a portal to an underground home!" The couple stared at her in horror.

"No, No!" the woman replied. "We have plans for an old-fashioned, plantation style home. We would never choose anything *this contemporary*!"

"Oh," Margo replied. "Still, you have to admit that the poem is intriguing." "You read the poem?" the man asked.

"Well . . . yes . . ." she stammered. "I mean, what kind of 'distant land' could be in a box?" They all thought for a moment. The men continued to struggle with the machinery. The man extended his hand to Margo, "Phil Peterson."

"Margo Ellis, pleasure to meet you," she offered.

"Mary," the woman smiled and nodded politely.

"'Distant land,' huh," Peterson muttered. "What if it contains ancient artifacts?"

"It probably got delivered to the wrong property," Mary volunteered.

"Delivered? What could have dropped this thing off? These guys haven't been able to move it a millimeter!" Phil answered. Margo finally got the courage to ask, "Have you all tried putting your hands on it?" Everyone fell silent for a moment. Individuals had halfheartedly tried putting their hands on it. People seem to have some fascination with fitting their hands into other people's handprints, like they do in the sidewalk in front of Mann's Chinese Theater in Los Angeles. But they had not tried doing it in unison. There were twelve sets of handprint insets: three on each side. Now that Margo had arrived, there were twelve people.

"This is preposterous," Peterson grumbled. "Of all the silly, cock-eyed . . ." Mary stopped him, "Phil, please, be polite. Margo is our new neighbor."

"No, of course, you're right," Margo answered. "It's all too far-fetched. Well, I'd better be going. It was nice meeting both of you. Good luck!" She ran back to her car and drove off to the grocery store, embarrassed for getting off on the wrong foot with her new neighbors.

That night, Margo had the strangest dreams. She dreamt of taking ships to distant lands. She found herself surrounded by opulence and friendly, smiling faces. Then, she'd be off on an airplane, and then a train. Each land that she visited was more beautiful than the next. She awoke the next morning with an intense desire to be near the big, mysterious cube.

While walking Franklin, Margo spotted the Petersons with an entirely new crew of workers, and with larger machinery.

"Good morning, Margo!" Mary shouted. Phil waved politely. Margo proceeded on her usual route, but an insatiable curiosity had her circle around and she retraced the path back to the Petersons's lot. The new crew and machinery were not able to budge the box either. *What was it about that thing? It couldn't possibly be too heavy to lift.* That equipment was probably sturdy enough to hoist a skyscraper! Could there possibly be a structure underneath that held it so securely to the ground? As she drew closer, she found that her suspicions were correct. The excavation revealed a solid metal foundation several meters into the ground. It wasn't going anywhere. The Petersons seemed both puzzled and disappointed. As each layer of dirt was removed, it revealed another measure of the metal foundation, and they grew more and more defeated. It was almost as if this structure grew up out of the ground overnight. Margo found herself feeling sorry for them. Franklin was quick to greet them and get acquainted. The three of them leaned on the Town Car, petting

Franklin, and watching in continual disbelief as the excavators dug deeper. Finally, Phil had had enough. He shouted and waved his arms, and told the men to quit working until he could figure out what to do next. The men welcomed the break. They sat, shaking their heads, and sipping their coffees.

Franklin ran circles around the cube, the men, and the neighbors. He amused everyone with his antics, and broke the tension among everyone. Eventually some of the men started horsing around, and dared each other to touch the box. When three of them touched the box on one side, it began to make a loud humming sound. Everyone was startled. They all looked at each other, as if to ask what to do next. Then, three more men came over, and the six men touched the box all at once. The two sides hummed in two harmonious sounds. Startled and laughing, everyone jumped back. "Well, I'll be damned," Phil uttered. He started toward the box, when Mary grabbed his arm, "Phillip, don't."

Three more workers started toward a third side of the box, and when the nine agreed to touch the box, three harmonious humming sounds emitted from the cube! The vibration rocked the ground, and Franklin leaped clear up into Margo's arms. All eyes fell on the neighbors. Everyone knew that if the mystery was to be solved, they too would have to lay their hands on the box. Peterson gave a nod, and a scaffold was lowered into the excavation hole and secured. Margo placed Franklin into the Town Car with Mary's permission, and then the three new friends proceeded onto the scaffold, to place their hands on the box. Sweaty, and hearts racing, they all agreed on the count of three to see what would happen if twelve people placed both hands on the box. The sound was a beautiful, harmonious hum, and the vibration was powerful; but this time, the sound was accompanied by a majestic rainbow of lights. It ended almost as quickly as it began, and the walls descended into the foundation, as a smaller, clear cube was revealed inside.

Etched in the clear walls were carvings of deer, sheep, horses, and mythological-looking creatures. More of the same cryptic lettering that was on the outer box was on the inner box, as well as some writing that could be understood by the awestruck twelve:

It is with great pleasure that we invite you to join us in humankind's predestined glory. If we are correct, then this vehicle has found its place in the year 2017. For further explanation, please read the enclosed letter. Once you are through, you will understand why we feel it is important for you to join us. Difficult times lie ahead for your planet. A solar eclipse will reveal instructions for transportation. To borrow one of your most appropriate phrases, Godspeed.

"What the hell?" Phil said disgustedly. He bent down and tried to reach the letter, which was positioned in a clear holder in the center of the cube. There was enough space for his hand underneath the clear wall, but not for his wrist or arm. Everyone bent down and tried to reach their hands underneath the walls, but no one's arm could fit. They all wondered how to get the letter. All attempts to retrieve it failed, including various tools and sticks. Eventually, curiosity gave way to frustration. Margo sat down on the scaffold. The Petersons and the workers all walked toward the machinery, trying to figure out what to do. Phil and Mary finally decided to send the crew home. There was no point in sticking around, trying to get this letter out of the cube. They needed time to think, and it was getting to be lunchtime. They decided to go and grab a bite to eat and figure out how they were going to incorporate this monstrous lawn ornament into the scheme of things for their new home. As Margo approached the car, Mary opened the door, and Franklin jumped out, and up into Margo's arms again. The Petersons asked Margo to join them for lunch, but she declined. She wasn't feeling well, and wanted to go home and lie down. After the crew and the Petersons drove off, Margo stood staring at the cube. This was the single most spectacular thing that had ever happened to her. *Could it be some kind of hoax? What could the makers of this box possibly hope to gain by getting people to believe that they would be transported somewhere by entering it? Perhaps it was all a joke for television. Was there a camera crew in the nearby woods? Why wouldn't they have come out by now?*

A full day had passed since she first spotted this thing. She wondered if it might be some kind of trap for a slavery or prostitution ring. She didn't think so. She sat on the ground, playing with Franklin, and thinking. Feeling rather tired, she lay on the grass, and wrapping Franklin up in her arms, fell asleep.

Margo awoke to something hitting her in the face. Franklin had the letter in his teeth! She sat straight up, yelling, "Where did you get that? How? Oh!" She realized that the wind must have blown the letter out of the bottom of the cube, which was open several centimeters on all sides except for the corners.

Why did everyone else leave? Wasn't this an extraordinary event in their lives, too? How could they possibly leave here? Margo found herself in a precarious situation. Should she read the letter? Technically, it belonged to the Petersons. *Or did it?* She thought about it for a good long while, and then decided to open it. She read the letter from beginning to end.

Chapter 2

The Letter

Day 1:

A gentle breeze blows through the open window of the sleeproom. The chatter of insects and breakday birds fills the air. There is a tranquil transition from slumber to wakefulness. I am completely immersed in gratitude for this ever-present peacefulness which is my life.

Filled with devotion to the One who created me, I give silent thanks and praise, pause to listen for guidance, then move to the children's rooms, where they too have slept peacefully and uneventfully all night. The one in my belly stirs and taps as if to want to wake her siblings, but the warm touch of my hand quiets and calms her. She'll have to wait until later to communicate with them.

I follow a sweet smell to the room you might call "kitchen," where Jeremiah, my homesteadman, has prepared a breakday meal. I find him in meditation and devotion. Our combined meditation almost seems to levitate us off the ground! As we finish, we are greeted by the children, eager to taste the foods whose aromas awakened them. But the animals must eat first.

My homesteadman, or "husband," as you might have called him, prepares us for our farming chores. Each of the children feed a different set of animals. These came to us from other worlds. Cayla, the oldest girl, feeds the blue lambs. Logan, the oldest boy, feeds the cows. Phoebe, the youngest, feeds the chickens. Jeremiah (Jerri) tills the soil, while I feed and groom the longhaired horses. We get cleaned up, and get ready for the breakday meal.

We bless it, and give thanks to the One, because we know that all good things come from this source. This is Planet Peace. We know that all who abide here are descendants of chosen ones from other planets. We have legends that tell us how their planets were devastated, and stories that warn us about misuse of our powers and resources. But we live in a state of continual bliss, where peace abounds, and happiness is pervasive. There is an inner contentment that seems so purposefully put there, as if earned as a badge of honor.

The children spontaneously clean up the meal room, and prepare for lessons. Some of these came from other worlds, and some were written by our elders. I teach them the history of the other worlds, and their minds are filled with wonderment. Their bright intellects cause them to question why the ones from previous planets misused their powers and resources. Why could they not trust and understand one another? Could they not hear each other's thoughts, as we do today? Would that not have eliminated most of the causes of their fears?

And why were insects, beasts, and pestilences allowed to harm them? We know no such things here.

Their questions cause us to want some fresh air and understanding, so we go outside and sit beneath our favorite tree. As we sit in meditation, we ask our ancestors to enlighten us and free us from our inquisitive thoughts.

Our collective meditation allows us to not only hear guidance, but to reveal a hologram of the deceased ones who came before. My grandsire, Eli, welcomes us with a warm smile, and reveals that he is very impressed with our questions. He asks that we pay close attention to his answers, and to those of the others who will accompany him. He warns that they are critical to our survival.

Eli asks his spirit guide, Jeredanglese, to inform everyone about the beginnings of the first civilizations. Jeredanglese agrees that this is an appropriate place and time for this discussion. He tells us that each of the early civilizations began much the same way as Planet Peace exists today. Inhabitants were deeply contented, and all was peaceful and well with these worlds. Creatures were tame, weather was tranquil, and pestilence was nonexistent. But the minds of the early inhabitants were weak, and eventually, they began to give in to fears. The fears were unfounded, but it seemed that they were contagious, so individual after individual would become fearful of one another, of beasts, of communities, of the weather, and of illness. This caused certain insects to grow stingers and other creatures to develop venomous qualities. This fearful time was what caused all manner of disease organisms to be born. Temperatures became extreme, rain became torrential, and wind became tornadic. The animal communities became restless and began acts of cannibalism. They ventured into the inhabitants' abodes and began attacking them as well. This was when the planetary ancestors and the beasts grew so-called "canine" teeth. With each of the planets, this was always a terrifying time. Fears were perpetuated into subsequent cultures and times. New fears about new beasts and diseases were rampant. That which was feared was actually created by preceding thoughts. The inhabitants never realized that their thoughts had created their realities. Jeredanglese warned that we should all take heed: that we guard our thoughts against fear; and life, as we know it now, will continue to exist.

Eli thanked him, as other elders began arriving. Their presence was comforting to all of us. It was so reassuring to know that we would reunite with these ones who came before, once we shed the current bodies that we now wear. In fact, it seemed to us that their very existence before our eyes was enough to make us never fear the end of life in the body. And knowing that we could call upon them at any time for guidance (or a reunion, as long as we were in a group) was a blessing beyond measure.

The elders praised us each individually, for the good works that we were doing, and the care that we were taking of each other and our creatures. They were pleased with the children's progress with the lessons, and with their telepathic talents. The occasional slipups could cause some sibling turmoil, but any unrest was usually resolved quickly and easily. It is easy to be a parent in this environment. I feel sorry for the parents in the old civilizations that had to contend with dangerous situations that their children might have encountered, on top of not knowing what was on their minds! I can hardly imagine life any other way than the way that it exists today! And while we are encouraged to learn about the past, the elders assured me that I am better off *not* imagining it at all!

Our ancestors asked if there were any more questions, and Phoebe popped up and asked if it was all right for her to be afraid of the fire in the hearth, or of falling off a cliff. The elders laughed and smiled and said that it was perfectly acceptable, as long as she did not "picture" getting hurt, or think about it for very long. We were instructed to recognize that simple dangers are a part of life, but they are never to be pondered or meditated on. Smiling and waving, they faded from our eyes. We were overwhelmed with joy at this visitation, and we ran back to share the news with Jeremiah.

In the meantime, the unborn sibling was leaping with joy, in the hope of recommunicating with the ancestors, and with her soon-to-be sisters, and brother. But now was her time to focus on the development of her body, and the children were so consumed with what they had learned, that they forgot to show her any attention today. She began kicking to show her disappointment. I called the children to her, and they began talking and singing to her. Her spiritual face appeared on my belly like one of your old "TV" screens! Cayla described her to me as cute and chubby. Logan informed me that she has bright, glowing eyes, and Phoebe said "Are we *sure* it's another girl?" We assured her that it was so, and she stomped off noisily.

Jerri asked what all the fuss was about, and the older ones told him of our visitation with the elders. They shared with him what they had learned about fears, and how they can be manifested into reality. The sire cautioned that we put these thoughts aside until another day, lest they find their way into our dreams. He said that he would like to invite some neighbors to the nightmeal, and I agreed that it would be nice for a change. We planned to prepare some steamed root vegetables and seasoned squash. Meat became available this night because an animal had crossed over. We are only permitted to eat animals if they die on their own, and not by our hand, so a meat meal is an uncommon event. Like our inhabitants, animals rarely ever contract diseases, and most die of old age, so the meat is always appropriate to eat.

Getting together with the neighbors is one of our favorite things to do. We laugh and share stories and play games and enjoy each other's company. The children picked fresh star fruits off the trees, then sliced them, and set them out on a platter. Jerri blessed the animal, then skinned and prepared the flesh, saving some in the ice cellar. I seasoned the cylinder squashes with salts and spices from previous planets: apsum, binkarum, cardamom, cinnamon, elano, and nutmeg, alphabetically. (We use the traditional "A to Z" alphabet because it's more versatile and practical than others). The beets and bush roots steamed in a pot over the hearth.

When our neighbors arrived, we placed their weather clothes on hooks and invited them in to share the warmth of our fire and friendship. We caught up on the latest news and information, such as the upcoming meetings, town gatherings, and celebrations. We shared stories of crop successes and failures, animal births and deaths, recipes and lesson plans. This brought the children to their most prized new story to tell: our visitation with the elders under the tree.

They shared with the neighbors our meeting with Jeredanglese and Grandsire Eli, and how they taught about fears. This led to a discussion about how fears perpetuated. Our neighbors spoke of learning about the inhabitants of previous planets, and how certain leaders learned how to utilize fear in others to increase their own financial gain and power.

Governments enjoyed when the inhabitants feared war, because it kept them in their leadership positions. Makers of weaponry, machinery, and vehicles enjoyed when they feared war because it kept them in business. Fuel companies enjoyed inhabitants' fears of running out of fuel, because they could raise the prices as they wished. Companies that made medicines enjoyed when inhabitants feared sickness and diseases, because they made them believe that they had all the answers to health. It was quite the contrary. While some of the medicines were made from natural ingredients and were helpful, most of them were made from chemicals and actually made inhabitants sicker! Fears made them keep taking more and more of them. Then the inhabitants became addicted to these products and couldn't stop themselves from desiring them. The neighbors learned that food-manufacturing companies did the same thing with their products. Foods were contaminated with addictive chemicals, and inhabitants couldn't help craving, purchasing, and consuming them.

Even churches instilled fears in inhabitants. They led their congregations to believe that they required the church in order to be received by the one at death. They took money from their congregations so they could prosper, grow, and compete with other churches. They altered sacred documents to further their own causes, and this in turn, caused countless inhabitants to be swayed in thought. We all fell silent for a moment to ponder what it must have been like to live in that time. Nothing could have been known as truth without telepathic communication and direct visitation from ancestors and elders. We all said a collective prayer of gratitude for our gifts of communication and truth.

Overall, our evening was a success, and our visit with the neighbors was enjoyable. We wished each other a pleasant evening, and promised to gather again soon.

Day 2:

While Planet Peace is an idyllic setting, it has its problems, too. We're still figuring out how to control our telepathy. If we don't practice quieting our thoughts, then others can receive too much information! And being in a crowd of inhabitants can be absolutely deafening, even if no one is talking!

We have our political debates, and sometimes the discussions of town appropriation of currency can get pretty tumultuous, but otherwise we have resolved most of what civilizations of the past used to dispute over.

Healthcare, for example, is a virtual non-issue. Basically, when one lives without fear, one lives without illness. We take very simple, consistent measures to insure the health of the body. Each abode has an herb garden filled with remedies, and every homestead member learns how to use them, in the event of illness or injury. Our culture was taught the true meanings and mechanisms of health and life by the chosen ones, removed from their planets, and we carry out those traditions today.

For example, we are taught that it is necessary for the core of the being to be in proper alignment in order for the body to function as it was designed. So inhabitants of Planet Peace get spinal alignments regularly, generally about once per week. This takes place from birth to death. We are also instructed by the early ones that the constitution of the being can use realignment, and so we all visit the herbalist at least once every year for an individualized remedy. And we have been taught the importance of rest, recreation, and enjoyment, so we do not take this instruction lightly. We are advised to quit our work as soon as the sun begins to descend, and to laugh and enjoy each other as much as possible.

We rub the muscles of the ones who have toiled the hardest first, and then we rub the muscles of everyone else afterward. We are told that this practice not only relieves pain, but is also essential to detoxify the body, so we are diligent in this tradition.

We eat what grows from the land in the season that it grows. There are no manufactured foods, as was the case on previous planets. It is forbidden to even store a canning beyond a year's necessity. We are advised to eat what grows within its season, in order to keep the body functioning at its fullest potential.

Inhabitants of Planet Peace sleep well and deeply, due to lack of fear, plenty of hard work, and play by day! Even if one should find oneself awake in the night, a remedy in the herb garden should suffice to bring a good night's sleep.

There are so many problems of the previous planets that have been resolved prior to the populating of Planet Peace. Poverty and hunger are nonexistent. Morals and education are dictated from the other side. Therefore, what is taught is ultimately and supremely overseen and approved by the One. This eliminates any confusion over what is true. We have learned that inhabitants of other planets spent their entire existences at war with their own planetary siblings over what they considered to be "right" or "wrong." We are blessed to have a steady stream of truth from the Source, and it is readily available to any of us at any time.

Inhabitants arrived here from many worlds, so we are visually extremely diverse. The skin colors are as many as the colors in our visible spectrum. There are so many colors that I am not sure that we even have names for all of them! There are at least fourteen blood types, and mostly everyone has pairs of eyes, ears, and limbs. Noses and mouths tend to be singular. Occasionally, there are antennae or tails, but they seem to be subsiding out of the collective gene pool. It has been 550 years now that this planet has been established. It was created to be a haven for souls who lived their previous lives to the highest potential. It was determined that the souls who strove to improve themselves in character and worked tirelessly to improve the lives of others were to be chosen to reside and retire here until the end of their days. This is the place which fulfills the "Thousand years of peace" prophesy. Peace and bliss fill our days and nights. We are truly blessed.

Planets from all the galaxies are constantly being observed by a Counsel of Elders in the heavenly dimensions. When the consciousness of the inhabitants of a planet reaches a certain level, significant changes begin to take place within their bodies, and within the planet. When life-forms increase their vibrational energy to a certain level, the monitoring of those life-forms by the Counsel begins.

It happens over eons of time. After the fears take over, inhabitants tend to become rather barbaric. They think only of themselves and their own betterment. As time goes on, they begin to think of the betterment of their immediate kin. The further passage of time allows some inhabitants to grow in maturity, realizing their connectedness to others, and striving for the survival and increased happiness of as many of their kind as possible. This growing altruism is one of the physical triggers of the geometrical prism. Each life-form has a geometrical prism, and each planet has a signature one, which is representative of the current level of consciousness present there. As *kindness* and *altruism* increase, so does the vibrational energy, and thus the geometrical prism changes shape.

The practice of meditation allows each individual prism to be seen clearly by the Counsel of Elders. Group meditations create group prisms. Likewise, group prayer creates a physical force field, but only when what is being prayed for is clearly visualized by all parties. The force field is extremely effective in achieving the desired outcomes, but it is group *meditation* that not only allows clear guidance, but also assures progenitous longevity: in a word, "rapture."

The early ones on each of the planets are largely unaware how their thoughts manifest into reality. Not only are fears detrimental, but negative thoughts of all kinds can inhibit one's life, one's consciousness, and contribute to planetary disharmony! Conversely, positive thinking is another one of the triggers of the geometric prism. Thoughts held in *positivity* and *faith* cause a polarization of electrons in the body's cells, thereby kick-starting the generator of the vibrational shape.

Finally, but most importantly, a devotional, loving connection to the One is the third and most crucial trigger for the shape. When one holds thoughts of *love* for one's Creator, one is assured of eventual participation in a prophesized time of peace.

This process has occurred in eons of time long before this one, and will occur again, and again, when the Counsel of Elders spot planetary geometric prisms that signal readiness.

Those who are qualified are assured participation in this process, whether they are in the life—or death-form, because we have full communication with those who cross over. Some in the heavenly dimensions choose to be born into a life-form on planets like Planet Peace in order to experience the true "Eden" promised to them on their former planet.

This was the case with Jerri and myself, our parents, our siblings, as well as our children, including this one who is yet unborn. She knew all that could be known in the heavenly realms, and she knew the bliss of heavenly existence. But one has only a brief opportunity to experience life simultaneous with complete peace, so she seized the opportunity! She and her angels and her spirit guides held a meeting, examining her former lifetimes, and agreed that she was worthy of this experience. She will be born soon. Gestational periods take one full year at this stage of DNA development. As consciousness increases on a planet, so do the number of DNA strands. By the time inhabitants are chosen for "rapture" from their planets, DNA strands are typically up to twelve in number. This process usually occurs so rapidly, that it escapes initial discovery by scientists. The bewilderment of the scientific communities of these civilizations generally becomes the impetus of the devastation of their particular planet.

Scientists who exhibit the three qualities of *altruism*, *faith,* and *love* of the One (and who consistently make regular meditative practices) become the calming, controlling, and leading forces among the faithful. Conversely, the *fear-based* scientific and religious communities usually begin a power struggle, and their attempts to control the masses with medications and threats ultimately lead to pandemics and pandemonium.

I do not recall the experiences of my previous lives on my former planet, Earth, because when we enter into life here, as with other planets, our memories are largely dampened. Occasionally, the children will recount memories of former lives, but the ability generally fades with age. The details that I am aware of regarding "rapture" are via the lesson plans, which I am given to teach the children. If anything about a lesson plan ever seems unclear, we are free to inquire of the elders, so that they may fill in the details.

Day 3:

I was informed when I was a child that I would write a long letter one day, and that it would be found by someone from Planet Earth. So when this Time Capsule project came up at the last town meeting, I immediately began to write. This is why my letter makes more references to Earth terms and customs versus those of other planets. It is also helpful that I had been given extra lessons in Earth life from my grandsire, Eli.

Grandsire Eli lived to be two hundred years old on Planet Peace, but I only got to enjoy forty years of his companionship here. He crossed over last year before my forty-first birthday, at his own request. We stay in communication with our angels and guides throughout our lives, and we participate in decisions about our life and death. He requested that his body be cremated, as most inhabitants do, and we all celebrated his return to the heavenly dimensions, in a customary ceremony. Grandmother Maria decided to remain here until our new baby is done nursing. She will move in with us to help with the homestead chores, and once the baby is weaned, she will reunite with Grandsire. We don't despair over these crossings, since we can communicate with anyone at will. And since my grandparents were direct descendants of Earth "people," I had the great pleasure of learning more about that planet.

"Rapture," as you can imagine, created a very confusing time on Earth. People were disappearing from society, and those without faith were in absolute hysteria. The geometric prism, which had formed around the planet, became an infrastructure for transportation. The geometric prisms, which had formed around individuals, became their transport "vehicles" within that infrastructure. The Governing Counsel, which oversees "raptures," sends liaisons to activate the prisms into transport mode. It is not known exactly how they do this, but it is believed to be accomplished by some type of "genetic switch." Perhaps I should explain more about the global process of "rapture" first.

It happens this way with all of the planets at the end of their time. While the collective consciousness of the masses is elevated, and *most* of the inhabitants exhibit the three qualities aforementioned, a small portion of the inhabitants grow comfortable and begin to revert back to the selfishness of the early years. The elevated collective consciousness changes the *shape* of the global prism. But as the young ones begin to show signs of the barbarism of some of their earliest ancestors, the planetary prism becomes *activated*. These younger ones give in to the pleasures of the body and to greed, which lead, karmically, to innumerable problems.

In the case of Planet Earth, "people" would give in to pleasures of food, for example. This would cause an endless number of diseases, and yet they would wonder why they end up so ill. They would give in to the pleasures of flesh in what they considered to be the "privacy of their homes" or in "harmless ways," and yet they wondered why unspeakable acts of fleshly crimes would be committed all over the planet. The inhabitants would amuse themselves with books and "TV" shows about murder, and then they would wonder why murder was so rampant on their planet. The majority of individuals never realized that every single act, and every single thought was part of an interconnected web: a matrix of consciousness.

But as mentioned earlier, there was a growing number of "people" who were exhibiting faith, love, and altruism. These individuals, whose prisms began to vibrate at higher levels, would experience increased intuitional senses. Angels and guides would telepathically lead them to right actions. The practice of meditation would enhance their "listening" ability, and the ability to heed right guidance. We are told that there are always unsavory entities, or "lost souls" who try to interfere with right communication, but regular practice of meditation enabled these humans to discern the saintly from the sadistic.

The people of Earth who were sensitive to the coming changes and faithful to the prophesy of "rapture" were given a name. They were called "lightworkers." This term came telepathically to some of the latter day prophets from angels and guides, who worked tirelessly in leading right action. Most of the early lightworkers never even knew why they were called by this term. But most knew instinctively when they belonged to this group.

It turns out that the term has a very literal meaning. Everything in the universe is made of light. Each particle, each element, and even each thought is made of light in a certain geometric shape, and vibrates at a certain frequency. If one had the most powerful microscope in the universe, one could see that the minutest particles, and even thoughts, have a certain color, shape, and pattern! These Lightworkers were purveyors of healing light, and they brought healing, hope, and transformation of the consciousness to the planet.

As planets approach the end of their time, there are usually wars going on, and they are generally caused by parties fighting over energy sources. On some planets, it was crystalline in nature, on others, a liquid mineral. On Earth, it was fuel known as "fossil," which means that it was created from the decayed bodies of beasts that lived eons of time before the humans.

Earth inhabitants naively trusted in an endless supply of fossil fuels, and their gluttonous greed led them to expend and waste energy supplies. The naiveté surrounding energy on Planet Earth seemed almost hypnotic. People very blindly trusted another form of energy known as "nuclear fission" that could actually cause the planet's destruction! Yet in spite of awareness of this fact, more and more nuclear power sites were built. It was known that a shift in tectonic plates (land below the surface of the Earth) could cause a quake that could rock a nuclear "reactor," and set off a series of dangerous explosions around the globe! But governments insisted that this form of energy was necessary, and so more reactor sites were created.

Lightworkers realized the extreme urgency for preparedness for an energy crisis. They demanded increased availability of "alternative" energy for the consumer. Ironically, "alternative" energies were the ones that were the *most available*! These were derived from the light of the planet's sun and from wind forces. Humans who had access to these types of energies never suffered, as did those who relied on conventional energy. The final days on planets usually result in the complete devastation of energy source sites. In this case, the Earth was covered in fire.

By the time the fires came, my Earth ancestors had been "raptured" off the planet. They were a mother, father, son, and daughter. The process of "rapture" could be very taxing to the human body. The journey through the vortex of space caused unconsciousness and required the human's angels and guides to be in a complete vibrational equipoise until the journey's end. The prism would then carry them safely to an Intergalactic Receiving Station, where family members would reunite, and healthcare was administered. Their stay was made as comfortable as possible, and they were constantly reassured that their kind deeds and thoughts on Earth had earned them a noteworthy retirement. They would be awarded a high-ranking status on a new planet and would be instrumental in the establishment of governmental, health, and educational structures there. They would be lavished with simple pleasures: plush beddings and furnishings, plentiful tasty foods, and entertainment. Special requests would be honored to the best of the welcoming staff's abilities.

This process usually proceeded uneventfully and without effort, except in the case of an individual who would arrive at the station alone, to find that none of their loved ones had qualified for "rapture." Severe depression and anxiety would ensue and would generally require a great deal of appeasement by the Governing Counsel. In extreme cases, a spiritual intervention would become necessary, where one would be permitted a visitation with deceased relatives and friends. If this process did not succeed in restoring the person to their normal senses and character, the Governing Counsel might recommend euthanasia, so that the human might enjoy a thousand years of peace from the heavenly realms.

Day 4:

Today I feel an unusual tingle, which signifies the readiness of our daughter to be born. It has been a full year since she descended into her physical body, and she has been working on its growth and development throughout the year. I will spend almost the entire day in meditation, until her arrival. The human female body of previous centuries would typically experience great pain in childbirth, but the genetic reshaping that arrived with the additional ten strands of DNA allows the birth process to proceed more easefully. The meditation process itself is also helpful in distracting from any pain that might have been felt otherwise. A small percentage of Earth women were aware of this, and they called the process "hypnobirthing."

Grandmother Maria is packing her things and getting ready to come over. She and my two sisters will be arriving shortly, bringing my two closest female neighbors with them. These five women will assist my daughter in her arrival, and take care of our needs by cooking, cleaning, and preparing herbs from the garden. Jerri and the children will remain outside the homestead today, paying extra attention to our animals by bathing and grooming them. Once our daughter is born, they will come inside, get cleaned up, and participate in her first birthday. Once she is bathed, and has her first breast milk meal, the entire family, along with friends, will sit in meditation, inviting the elders to our celebration. When the elders arrive, via hologram, they will give us her name, and they will share with us some of her past life triumphs and tragedies, as well as some of her strengths and potentialities. We will enjoy an extensive feast prepared by the women and spend the evening getting acquainted with our newest family member.

Later:

It has been a blessed and wonderful day. The birth proceeded as easily as I had predicted, and all went according to plan. Grandmother Maria prepared a calming tea for all of us to share, and we enjoyed each other's company until it was time for me to go so deeply into meditation that I did not even know who was present. I felt a deep, strong connection to the Divine, and a comforting calm blanketed me, as our daughter passed easily from the warm pool that she has known all year, to a warm bath that I had been placed into. She swam to the surface with a peaceful smile on her face, and Jerri and the children arrived just in time to greet her! We all bonded with her instantly, and she cooed as she took her first meal. We all snuggled close together under one large blanket, as my relatives and neighbors gathered in the "kitchen" to prepare the big meal.

Everything that was prepared was warm and delicious, and afterward, we all sang soft lullabies until all the children were asleep. This is how I am able to be with you now in my letter. Just before the slumberers fell asleep, the ancestors arrived to give us the name of our new daughter. She was given the name "Deidre," which means "youngest daughter."

We were told that she will change her name when the time comes, and that I will give birth to more children in the future, but they will all be sons, thus her name will be appropriate.

The ancestors told us that Deidre is a strong and capable soul. She enjoys being challenged to new levels of ability, endurance, and maturity. She has been spiritually perfecting herself for a long time, and she has devoted most of her lifetimes in the service of others. She has been a slave and a slave owner, a peasant and an aristocrat, a servant and a celebrity. As a male, she had occupations in everything from construction to politics. As a female, she worked hard as a seamstress, but in another life, enjoyed the "good life" as a well-adored movie star. We are told that we have seen her perform in some of our broadcasted productions. Perhaps I should explain what that means.

You see, while this is the future, relative to your current time and place, we do not have television or movies, as you know them. While our knowledge and capability of technology is far more advanced than yours, we live simply and even "primitively" compared to the culture as you know it.

It is mandated by the Counsel of Elders that we live this way in order to experience true peace, the way life is intended to be. We experience entertainment following our town meetings, via a group meditation, which brings a hologram of plays from the beyond. We are rewarded for our efforts at making Planet Peace a better place to live by watching performers who have transitioned to the other side. These are very often the most qualified and talented performers of the centuries of time, all coordinated by the most talented directors, writers, and producers of all time. The productions are meaningful to all of us who abide here, young and old, and tell stories in themes that have been repeated throughout the ages. We are blessed to receive this entertainment, and we gratefully acknowledge all who are responsible for the productions.

So it turns out that Deidre has actually performed for us in one or more of these productions! Our dear little "starlet!" She is beautiful, with a pale, pink, rosy glow to her chubby cheeks, and her blue eyes show joy, gratitude, and intelligence. We are told that she will be a hard worker at the homestead, but she will also show great courage and fortitude at the end of our time of peace. We are not permitted to know what happens at the end of these ages of peace, but we do not fear it, because we know and trust the One who created us.

Day 5:

It occurs to me on this day that I may have confused you about the concept of a time capsule. Time capsules were traditionally placed in the ground of a planet, for the purpose of educating later generations about the earlier ones. This one, which contains my letter, has been strategically sent back in time to Planet Earth to the year 2017, in the hope that it will be used in the year 2018. Our numerologists and scientists agreed that this was best because the numbers totaled to "eleven." Eleven is a "master number," which means that it is an auspicious time for spiritual awakening. The intention behind the time capsule is to educate the people of the planet in order to prepare them for "rapture." This is a final attempt to assure that as many inhabitants as possible exhibit the qualities of faith, love, and altruism, and make a daily practice of meditation, including group meditation, whenever possible. My letter is intended to bring hope as well as guidance.

Later:

Cayla and Logan brought my breakday meal into the sleeproom. They were happy to see their new sibling "in person" after a full year of viewing her on my "TV screen" belly. They played with her and sang to her, as Deidre studied their faces. She stared at Cayla's black hair, strong cheekbones, and lavender eyes. She grabbed at Logan's long brown hair, and poked his dark eyes. Phoebe was peeking in from the doorway, half-hoping to be seen. It was clear that she needed some attention. I sent the eldest ones to help their sire, and invited Phoebe in. She got into the bed, opposite her new sister. She ran her fingers through her short blonde hair, and glanced at the ceiling. I asked Phoebe what she would like to say. She thought for a while, and then asked, "How can you possibly love *all* of us?" I put my arms around her and told her that nothing could ever stop me from loving her or make me love her less. "In fact," I told her, "each day that I spend with you, and get to know you better, makes me love you all the more!" Phoebe seemed incredibly relieved. Then she asked, "Will you love Deidre more each day, too?" "Yes," I replied. I could see that it was time to "paint the big picture" for her. I explained to Phoebe that the One has more children than it is possible to count, and yet the One never runs out of love. It is the same with parents. We are taught that just as the universe expands, so does love. Goodness and love actually grow and expand with space.

During the thousand years of peace, inhabitants are largely protected from "heartache." It is possible to get into disagreements with one another, but peace pervades, and love abounds to the extent that it is almost palpable. Angels and guides are very present in our lives as well, so their intervention is almost immediate during disharmony. We are told that this type of intervention is possible on Planet Peace, as well as other "rapture refugee" planets, because of the way that the matrix of space is stretched around the planet.

But we have learned that heartache had its place in former civilizations. The deeper one is hurt, the deeper one is capable of love. The more pain one experiences in life, the greater the gift of being pain-free, even if the release from pain does not occur until death. To the human mind on Earth, this concept often seemed unfair and incomprehensible. Earth teachers from all generations and all "corners" tried to teach this concept. But the experience of consciousness within the body would often cloud the judgment and prevent philosophical exploration of such concepts. Humans often sought "quick-fix," solutions such as pain relievers and guilt-ridden pleasures. Some even brought about their own death prematurely with suicide. This brings great sorrow to the One: rejection of the gift of life. Space is endowed with a matrix of opportunities for each of us. No situation is ever so desperate that it is without hope. Positive thoughts and prayers, both private and collective, will always bring about positive changes. This is the mechanism that is set in place by the One, for the benefit of all of his/her children. It is a sad fact that many of the suicide victims on Planet Earth killed themselves over what they thought was the "love of their life," when that which they were seeking had not yet arrived.

When an individual truly communicates with the One, through prayer and meditation, he or she knows of the vast, unending love for all of "God's children." In the case of Earth, humans who truly communicated with the Divine knew that all humans deserved to live completely free from harm. If all on Earth had done this, there would be no "sibling rivalry" among Earth children, who all came from an original set of parents, essentially. There simply is no "us" and "them." There is only one continuous, expansive spirit.

But the Earth, like all the other planets in all the other galaxies, had its story to live out. There would be those who would never comprehend that humans have the right to live unharmed. And so, harm was done. But heed my letter: *those need not be you*! We enjoy every soul who joins us here on Planet Peace. Each being brings some characteristic to our existence here. We would be blessed to have more of you with us!

This time capsule is an experiment with the space/time continuum. The Town Counsel wanted to see if we could have some Earth inhabitants make a leap from their parallel universe to ours. The success of this project means that humans living in the year 2018 will arrive into our teleportation device on Planet Peace. They would actually bypass the "rapture" process initiated by the "liaisons," and simply teleport here.

Our scientists invented a teleporter that could be activated by several people who exhibit the three qualities of faith, love, and altruism, and with their individual prisms activated by a group meditation, the teleporter would transport them directly here. Unfortunately for them, they would have missed out on the first 550 years of peace, but better late than never!

Once the humans arrive here, inhabitants from Planet Peace would be responsible for orientating them to their new surroundings. The townspeople have been building homesteads and preparing farms for the new arrivals.

We aspire to be as welcoming to our new neighbors as the welcoming committees of the Intergalactic Receiving Stations. The Counsel of Elders gave their approval for this project, and promised to be of assistance if any newcomers act strangely. Many of our historians are fluent in several languages, and are prepared to communicate and to translate in the event that the arrivals speak something other than the English language, the primary language on Planet Peace.

The stretched matrix around our planet is the mechanism, not only for angelic intervention, but also for our telepathy. It activates the portions of the brain which are considered to be "unused" while inhabiting Earth. So our new neighbors will be introduced to the world of telepathy rather suddenly, and may be overwhelmed! Our welcoming committees are prepared to share our ample supply of calming teas, herbs, and foods, as well as plenty of reassurance that telepathy *can* be managed! We have gathered provisions, rehearsed several dialogues, and readied ourselves for various outcomes for several months now. We feel quite prepared for our new guests!

A hospitality wing has been added to the Town Hall, and murals of Earth cities have been painted on the walls, to make our guests feel at home. The cooking staff has been practicing ancient earth recipes, and the sewing committee has been preparing bedding, curtains, and clothing representative of the Earth era 2018. Books and relics, representative of the time, have been placed in the hospitality wing. Our historians have been working diligently to replicate as many aspects of our newcomers' era as possible. Our psychologists will be among the first to greet the new arrivals. Groups of angels will be present to expand the grace and harmony of the atmosphere, although the newcomers will not be likely to see them at first.

Day 6:

Jerri has just arrived home from a town meeting, and all of the greeting and hospitality committees are reporting a readiness for the release of the time capsule. They asked how my letter was coming along, and he assured them that I was working on it daily. The scientists will inscribe step-by-step instructions on the teleporter, but my letter is meant to be an incentive for the Earth people to get inside and "give it a whirl!"

As I mentioned earlier, our goal is to retrieve as many Earth people as possible from the planet. The devastation that lies ahead is unfathomable. But the One has great mercy, so we are permitted to free as many as we possibly can from the unspeakable punishment of continued life on Earth. I am not permitted to go into further detail except to say that light, clean air, clean water, and food will be frightfully scarce, and that even blinking and breathing would be incessantly painful. Pestilence, disease, and fire will abound, and the portal for "rapture" will be closed to those who attempt to ameliorate too late.

With that being said, those whom we aspire to be able to retrieve will obviously be open-minded! Teleportation devices on Earth will not even be considered a possibility, until long after 2018. So the brave souls who step inside will definitely be of strong will and fortitude! We are hopeful that we may be able to convince some of the deeply religious that it is safe to meditate. We would be blessed to teach some people that it is appropriate to give of themselves freely (altruism). We also hope that some who are devoted to the One can realize that if they simply catch their negative thoughts, and turn them around into positive ones, they can experience the predestined joy of the ages (faith)! We are even hopeful that the lost souls, who are fatally optimistic and trust that "mankind" will save itself from destruction, will learn to put their trust, faith, and love into the One who created them (love).

We hope to cast our net and catch some fish with singular flaws: the ones who would have *almost* qualified for "rapture," and help them to avoid an end of unsurpassed misery.

We understand that humans may feel some hesitation in entering a transport vehicle to a distant place in the future. Your history is fraught with stories of alien abductions and the atrocities of alien surgical exploration. There was an abrupt end to those stories, though, which most of you did not notice, as Intergalactic Counsels put a strict end to those abductions.

It did not stop the visitation by spacecraft, as your alien brothers and sisters tried to communicate with you and get you to realize that they existed!

We don't want you to feel as though any malice or wrongdoing will come to you by entering this vehicle. If you are one who meditates regularly, you will know this intuitively via your meditation. Once you realize that it is safe to enter, you may know that it is a vehicle to your eternal freedom. Know that bliss and joy await you, that you will live longer and healthier and happier in an eternal haven of joy, wonder, and merriment.

Another point which I would like to make is that you can rest assured that all will be properly cared for here. By now, some of your elderly and mentally ill have been "raptured" from hospitals and retirement homes. When they arrive at the Intergalactic Station, they are detained in its medical facility and evaluated. Their bodies are detoxified from the poisons and chemicals, which made many of them sick in the first place, and most of them gain awareness and clarity within the first twenty-four hours. Once detoxified, it is determined which herbal remedies are appropriate replacements for their current medications, and they proceed on to Planet Peace's retirement habitations. For the small percentage who remain incognizant after detoxification, an angelic intervention is performed to facilitate the miracle of their healing. In a rare instance where a miraculous healing is not permitted the Counsel might recommend euthanasia, to ensure their enjoyment of the thousand years of peace from the heavenly realms. For those of you who are still unaware of the afterlife, the astral body has total health and clarity in heaven. There, they may also become eligible for birth onto Planet Peace.

You may also be aware of the "rapture" of certain children from slavery, abduction, and orphanage settings. They, too, are properly cared for. After their arrival onto our planet, they go immediately to our childcare facilities where they are free to create, explore, learn, and play as they wish. Their care is overseen primarily by the monks and the nuns whose "raptures" preceded theirs, and, whenever possible, they are reunited with their biological parents, even if they had never met on Earth! The reunion is usually a blissful one, with angels expanding the harmony of the atmosphere, and the bonding is generally immediate among family members.

So you have some choices to make regarding this opportunity. You can perfect your qualities and characteristics to the extent that you may take a "free ride" into the future, or you may take your chances with life on Earth, and hope for the best. The best would be that you perfect your qualities and meditation talents in the hope that a liaison will find you and assist you with your "rapture" in the very near future. Conditions on Earth will begin to deteriorate from this point on. If you choose to remain, you may regress in your qualities, letting fear and greed become your motives. This would deactivate your personal prism, and the liaisons would surely be unable to find you.

Your first reaction, after reading this letter, will probably be one of mistrust and uncertainty. If you are an intuitive human, you will probably start sharing the news with your loved ones first, and then with those with whom you are in immediate contact. If you are an evolved being, ready for "rapture," you will probably begin recruiting as many as possible to read copies of this letter, and have people standing in line at the teleporter daily, as you shepherd them to their merciful destiny.

Whichever path you choose, all that I have left to say is that I bless you on your path, wish you a safe and pleasant journey, and look forward to (hopefully) meeting you very, very soon. Incidentally, my name is Rebecca Home.

Chapter 3

Potluck

Impossible, she thought. *How could this be?* True, there was an energy crisis, and she thought that she had heard something on the news about the discovery of additional strands of DNA, but how crazy would that be?

Margo began to take an inventory of her life. Was she altruistic? She liked to think of herself as being generous. Did she have faith in and love for God? She did. Was she a meditator? Usually, only during yoga. Would this qualify her for "rapture"? She wasn't sure.

If she did decide to go into the vehicle, what would become of her children, Franklin, and her house? She reasoned that the latter would be inconsequential if the predicted changes were to come true. She would have to make sure that her children had the three qualities and that they learn to meditate. Good qualities were hard to find in them after they spend the weekends with their father. Margo and her husband had been separated for six months. He was living in an apartment in town. *Funny*, she thought to herself, *I don't really care if* he's *got the three qualities! The "qualities."* What was she thinking? *This is nonsense!* Still, there was something about that letter and its author. She could *feel* her *integrity*.

Margo and Franklin headed home. Margo had stuffed the letter into her back pocket, reasoning that if she had put it back, the wind would have blown it out of there again. She vowed to herself to bring it back to the Petersons tomorrow, hoping they would understand why she took it.

Margo fed Franklin and made herself a sandwich. She couldn't stop thinking about the letter. She started judging all of her actions mentally, asking *was that altruistic?* or *is that acting in faith?* She picked up the phone and started calling some neighbors and friends, inviting them to come over for a potluck dinner. She planned on telling them of her experiences, and showing them the letter. She hoped that they wouldn't think she was crazy. This was Friday, and her husband would be picking the kids up from school for the weekend.

Katie was fifteen and Jonathon was eleven. Basically they were good kids. They did well in school and stayed out of trouble for the most part. On Sunday nights, however, they would come home like a pack of starving wolves: fighting with each other and Margo about everything, it seemed. This was how things were with her husband. It was also the primary reason for their separation. Matt was very opinionated and bossy. He was never abusive, but it was tiresome to fight all of the time. Margo felt that some time apart would do them good.

At 2:00 p.m., the doorbell rang. "Speak of the devil," Margo muttered. She opened the door, and Matt walked in. "Nice of you to ring the bell," Margo said.

"I didn't want to scare you," Matt answered. "I just came to pick up some of the kids' warmer clothes in case we go camping. Do we still have sleeping bags?" he asked.

"In the basement," she answered. This was going well. Should she push it and tell him what happened? He would likely turn irrational about it. But he was being so nice today, and she really needed to talk to someone about this.

"Matt, I need to talk to you, do have a few minutes?" Margo asked.

"Sure. What's up?" he responded.

"I have something *incredible* to tell you. I've *got* to tell someone about this, but you have to promise to stay *calm,* and to *believe* me. Do you promise?"

"What's going on, Margo?" His tone was getting louder and more serious.

"Matt, are you going to be civilized here, because I really need a friend right now," she said exasperatedly. He sensed her sincerity, and realized that he had an opportunity to exercise patience, as he had promised so many times to do. So very calmly, he stated, "OK, I'm sorry, go on."

"Something amazing has happened. It was like out of a movie, or something. I *swear,* Matt, everything that I am about to tell you is true. Please promise that you'll believe me!"

Matt knew that his wife was sensible. In fact, he believed her to be the most sensible person that he knew. He knew that he wanted things to be better between Margo and him. He wanted his family back. If she needed a friend this desperately, then he would drop everything to be there for her.

"Relax," he said, "I'm listening. I'm all ears, and I promise to believe everything that you say. So what happened?"

Margo proceeded to tell Matt everything that had happened, including her dreams. He stared in amazement. Matt knew that Margo was a skeptical person.

She had a scientific mind, was great with numbers, and refused to read editorials or horoscopes. She would be the *last* person to ever conjure up a fantasy to get attention. That could only mean one thing. What had happened to Margo was real.

"I believe you," he said.

She immediately began to cry. Another human being validated her experience, and didn't try to figure out how it might be a sham. She handed Matt the letter, and he began to read. When he was through, he looked up at Margo and said,

"So what do we do?"

Margo was suddenly finding herself on all sorts of unfamiliar territory. First of all, her husband was being understanding and supportive! At the same time, she realized that she was actually contemplating taking a vehicle into the future! She wasn't sure if her heart was pounding so hard because she was so scared, or because she was falling in love with this man all over again!

"Let's see if Mom can take the kids tonight," she said. "I have people coming here, and I can use your help."

"I'm on it," he replied.

One by one, neighbors started arriving with casserole dishes and plate warmers. Margo had set out some paper plates and napkins, while Matt picked up the kids' clothes and books from the family room. She lit some candles and put on some music, while he pulled a few bottles of wine out of the pantry. The friends and neighbors began to wonder if this gathering was an announcement that they were reuniting. One thing was for sure; something was suddenly different between them.

When the last had guest arrived, Margo found her heart racing. She realized that she *had* to tell them what had happened. It was her duty to report the events, no matter how they would be received. She gulped down her wine and said, "OK, here goes. I've invited you all here tonight to share with all of you something incredible that happened to me today."

"You won the lottery!" quipped Candy, her closest neighbor.

"No," Margo responded.

"You got a job!" said her sister, Vickie, sarcastically.

"No! Look, don't guess. I just have to tell you," Margo interrupted. "You need to listen to this because it really happened, and I'm not crazy, and it's really extraordinary, and I don't know what to do!"

She told them the story of the mysterious metallic box and the letter. Candy's husband, Mike, said, "May I read the letter?"

Candy said," It's probably just a very talented architect, or some freak trying to scare people."

"You need to get some engineers out there to take the thing apart, and maybe some forensic scientists to figure out who put it there," said Jodi, Margo's former college roommate.

Mike's sister, Barbara, said, "What if it's real?"

"Oh, come on!" Vickie answered. "I'll take my chances and stay here!"

"But are you meditating? Do you have the qualities?" Barbara questioned.

"I'll work on it," retorted Vickie.

Barbara continued, "But what if it gets really bad, I mean politically, and what if all kinds of wars and famines and epidemics break out?"

Vickie blurted out, "You have an overactive imagination!"

Candy said, "Let's eat, I'm starved!"

Matt sat quietly in the corner, listening and taking in everyone's comments. He made eye contact with Margo, and the look was intense. She could tell that he believed her. He knew that she was very practical and sincere. He knew that she did not give in to flights of fancy. He also sensed the integrity in Rebecca's letter.

Mike turned to Matt and said, "Did you read this?"

"Yeah," Matt replied.

"What do you make of it?" Mike inquired.

"I don't know, man, but I know one thing: Margo has never been this serious about anything before. I believe her, and I think I believe this letter. We need to see if we can gather a few more details, and figure out what to do," Matt said.

As the evening progressed, the conversations turned away from the events of the day to more mundane topics. Talk of carpools, children's grades, neighbors' landscaping, and sports injuries replaced the single greatest spectacle that Margo had ever seen. She listened as everyone droned on, wondering how they could obsess over such trivial matters, while the greatest dilemma of their time stood staring them in the face.

As she stood there, staring at everyone in a low level of shock, her dear friend Abby lovingly placed an arm around her. "Margo," Abby said, "I have been pleading with you for ages now to embrace this idea. In The Revelation, chapter 14, verse 7: 'For the time has come when he will sit as Judge. Worship him who made the heaven and the earth . . .'" Abby was a devout Christian. Margo was raised in Christian religion, but she had so many doubts. Mostly, she doubted the man-made rules and regulations which seemed to have no biblical foundation, and she also doubted the gospel translations. She and Matt used to stay up late at college and discuss their views on these matters. Their common skepticism seemed to draw them closer together. They met Abby when they were all majoring in business at Penn State University.

The guests began cleaning up and gathering their things. They said their good-byes and assured Margo that there was some logical explanation for her remarkable experience. She smiled and nodded, feeling betrayed by each one of them. Abby was the last to leave. She turned at the doorway and said, "You know, you can turn your back on this whole experience, and just follow the Lord."

"I know, Abby, thanks, and good night," Margo replied, knowing in her heart that she *was* following the Lord.

Matt said, "Well, I'd better be going, too . . ."

"No," Margo stopped him, "Please stay."

Chapter 4

To Tell the Truth

Margo popped one eye open enough to see the clock; it was 9:40 a.m.! She threw the covers back and scrambled around frantically, pulling on her jeans and jacket. Running down the stairs and out the door in her slippers, she sprinted down the road with the letter in her hand.

Franklin greeted Matt with his leash in his teeth. Matt groaned and rolled over, but Franklin met him on the other side of the bed, panting excitedly. Matt suddenly realized that Margo must have gone to return the letter, so he dressed quickly and bounded down the stairs and out the door, Franklin galloping behind him. The two jogged down the road, finding Margo in a heated argument with the Petersons. Matt could see in the distance that Mr. Peterson was yelling at Margo, waving his arms in the air and stomping the ground. Mrs. Peterson was trying to calm him down. Margo was clearly apologizing, but to no avail. Police cars and forensic lab vans surrounded the property, and yellow crime scene tape formed a perimeter around the cube.

"You must be Mr. Peterson," Matt introduced himself.

"Who the hell are you?" Peterson responded.

"I'm Matt Ellis, Margo's husband. I've heard nice things about you," Matt said, trying to smooth things over.

A police officer approached the group. "Do you know these people?" he asked the Petersons.

"Yeah," Peterson responded, "*She* had the *letter*!"

"But I brought it back!" Margo shouted.

"You touched that?" the officer asked Margo, "Ma'am, do you realize that this is criminal evidence?"

"Criminal? What crime was committed?" Margo asked.

"Trespassing and vandalism for starters," the officer replied.

Matt said to Margo, "Look, Babe, maybe we'd better go."

The officer stopped them, "Excuse me, we're going to be needing a statement from you, uh, Mrs . . . ."

"Ellis," Margo answered.

Matt took Margo aside saying, "Listen, I don't think this is a good idea."

A large truck whizzed by and stopped a few feet away from them. It was a local news truck. Reporters and cameramen poured out and began setting up their equipment. The reporters approached the police cars with clipboards in their hands. The officer took Margo into a squad car, while more news vans pulled up. Matt felt sure that this would not end well. He wished that he had brought Franklin's leash. He was running up to meet all the police officers and news personnel, as well as running circles around the cube. All attempts to catch him failed. He was having too much fun.

Margo reported everything as it had happened to the officer.

"Thank you, ma'am," he said. She felt like an idiot. What kind of a person in her right mind reports a story like that to a police officer?

"May I go?" she asked.

"Don't leave the premises," he responded.

Margo joined Matt and Mrs. Peterson. Mary apologized for her husband's rude behavior. Margo said, "No, Mary, it's OK. I understand why he was mad. He didn't know that I had every intention of returning the letter."

"So, Margo, what did it say?" Mary asked.

"Oh, Mary, it's very compelling! It's written by a woman named Rebecca, and, well, I made copies last night. I'll bring you one!" Margo replied.

"Thank you, I'd appreciate that," Mary responded. She seemed a bit distracted because she could see Phil in the distance, screaming at a police officer the same way that he had screamed at Margo. "Excuse me," Mary said, as she made her way toward her husband and the officer.

A reporter approached Margo, asking her to make a statement for TV. Matt gave her a look that said, "You'd better not do this," but Margo agreed. Something inside her was telling her that this was important, and that people would need to know the truth. They could decide for themselves whether or not to believe it, but she felt compelled to tell the truth. Margo told the reporter what had happened the previous days, and then she repeated her story again to a live television camera. Matt was trying to figure out what they were going to tell their children. He could just imagine how furious they would be when they found out that their mother was on TV, embarrassing them to death. He could also imagine his parents rolling their eyes, and saying, "I told you so," regarding his wife.

But Matt knew that he must defend Margo. He knew her to be a smart and sensible person, no matter what others might think. When Margo was through with her statement, she picked up Franklin and headed over to Matt. "The officer says that I'm free to go now," she said.

"Good. Are you hungry? I'll make us some breakfast," Matt replied. Margo welcomed the invitation, and they headed home.

Matt had missed making breakfast for this family. He made pancakes, eggs, and toast, while Margo brewed some coffee for the two of them. They discussed how they would prepare the children for the attention they might get because of their mother being on TV. "We could tell them, 'Kids, we've got good news and bad news. The bad news is that Mom is crazy as a loon, and everyone in town is about to know it. The good news is Mom and Dad are back together!" Margo joked.

"Or," Matt interjected," we could sneak them off to Aruba and tell them there!"

"Not a bad idea," Margo agreed. The phone rang suddenly, and Margo answered it. It was the police officer who had taken her statement.

"Mrs. Ellis?" he asked.

"Yes," Margo replied.

"This is Officer Michaels from the Bucks County Police Department," he said.

"Oh, hello," she said.

"Ma'am, we detected some radioactivity on the Petersons's property around the perimeter of the cube. The cube itself and the letter don't show any radioactivity, but the ground surrounding the area is highly radioactive. We're going to need you and your husband to come down to the hospital and meet us outside the emergency room entrance. Oh, and you'll need to bring your dog, too," he said.

"Right now?" she asked.

"Yes, immediately," he answered.

"OK, we'll be right there," Margo said. "Come on," she told Matt, and grabbing Franklin, "I'll explain in the car."

The police were waiting for them at the hospital, and escorted them to an underground laboratory. They were each scanned for radioactivity, and found to be free of contamination.

"They're all clear," one officer said.

"I don't get it," Officer Michaels queried. "How can there be all that radioactivity in the ground and none on the people standing on it? It's like this thing came up from the ground!"

"That's what I thought," Margo interrupted. "Does that mean that the Petersons and all of the workers are OK too?"

"Yeah," Michaels answered, "everyone is OK."

"Oh, thank God," Margo responded. "I thought I was going to have to call everyone who read the letter at my potluck dinner last night, and have them all come down here."

"You let people read that letter?" Michaels asked.

"Of course," Margo answered.

"We're going to have mass hysteria on our hands," Michaels said. "We'd better keep a twenty-four-hour watch on this thing," he added, dialing his chief on the phone.

"Excuse me," Matt asked, "are we free to go?"

"Yeah, you can go," Michaels answered, "but don't leave town."

"There goes Aruba," Margo frowned.

Chapter 5

A Family Reunited

Matt went back to his apartment to pack up a few things to bring back to the house. As he packed, he began to take stock of this life. Before meeting Margo, he was considered to be a lady's man, dating beautiful women, mostly for sport. Back then, he wasn't very honest, or reliable, or even friendly, but meeting Margo seemed to change all of that. He found that he was inspired to be a better person around her. Matt's friends even told him that they liked the change that had come over him, because he was more dependable and trustworthy. The early years of his marriage were fun. He and Margo both made good money in accounting and investments, and they were able to build the home of their dreams. His promotions enabled Margo to quit her job and stay at home with the kids, although she worked part-time from home just to have a little extra spending money.

As the children started maturing into adolescence, Matt found himself slipping back into his old ways. Raising the children became more challenging, and he found himself acting like his own father. Suddenly, there was a lot of yelling in the house and tempers would fly out of control. Matt now realized that he was simply using the parenting skills that he was taught by example. But he also noticed that his temperament would affect all areas of his life, and he knew that it had to change now.

He began to examine his life to see if he had all of the "qualities." Thanks to Margo, he had grown closer to God, because she acquainted him with spirituality and introduced him to their current church. He had been uncomfortable with the religious concepts and man-made rites of the religion he was born into. Matt found that he could connect to his Creator with prayer and in solitude, and enjoyed learning to become a better person via studying their spiritual philosophies, and applying them to their lives. So, as for the quality of loving God, he knew that he at least had that one.

Matt knew that believing in God was one thing, but trusting in God was quite another. It was difficult, particularly coming from a family of worriers, to trust that everything would always turn out all right. But his spiritual teachings had caused him to strengthen his faith, and so he felt fairly secure in the second quality.

As for the quality of altruism, Matt believed himself to be quite generous. After all, his taxes showed that, right? He realized, however, that he could probably extend his kindness to others a little more broadly.

Meditation was an area in his life that would require some work. Every time he tried to meditate, he found it difficult to quiet his thoughts. He would find himself thinking of work, or his most recent argument with Margo, or the kids. Matt resolved to get better at this practice as he did with the other areas of his life. He threw his suitcase in the car, and drove home, feeling more hopeful and happy than he had felt in a long time.

Arriving back home, Matt found Margo in a panic.

"Matt, what are we going to tell the kids?" She pointed to the TV which was already broadcasting the cube story. The footage showed Mr. Peterson ranting at a police officer and pointing to the big metal box. Then Margo's face appeared across the screen, telling her testimony of the past day's events. The reporter finished with, "Well, that's what's happening in Bucks County, PA, back to you, Jim."

Margo was seriously regretting her decision to tell the truth to the reporter. She and Matt had very little time before the children would be home, and she was very concerned about the repercussions of this broadcasted news. It was even beginning to show up on different channels!

"Look, stay calm, we'll figure something out," Matt assured her. "Besides," he said, "what's the worst that can happen?"

Just then, the phone rang, and it was Margo's parents. "Yes, I've seen it, yes, it's true . . . No, I'm not . . . No, listen, I'm telling you it really happened, OK? I don't care what the neighbors will think, this is *real*, Mom!" Margo slammed the phone down. As she stared at Matt, tears began to roll down her face. She wanted Matt to say that everything would be all right and that all of this attention would go away. But in her heart, Margo knew that this was the single most important thing that had ever happened to any of them, and she knew that no matter what the neighbors, relatives, or community had to say, this was a wake-up call to humanity. She could feel it to the core of her body.

Matt said, "OK, let's decide how we're going to tell the kids about all of this," and the two of them prepared some of the dialogue that they would have with their children. Margo's mother had promised to have them home before dinner.

When Katie and Jonathon came home, they were pleasantly surprised to find their parents home together, and their dad's suitcase at the bottom of the stairs. They guessed correctly that he was moving back in, and Katie squealed, while Jonathon said, "All Right! I knew it!"

What they didn't know was that their parents were about to lay a heavy burden on their shoulders. Matt and Margo prepared them for the worst, as they explained all that had happened, up to the moment. The children remained quiet and stunned. It was a lot to handle all at once. They read the letter on the couch in the family room.

"Mom, what are we going to do?" Katie asked.

"We need to talk to Reverend Sal," Margo answered. "I think that will help to sort things out for us."

"Can we go live under a rock somewhere for a while?" Jonathon asked.

"We actually thought of that," Matt answered, "but unfortunately we're required to stay in the area."

"Can we please be home-schooled?" Katie asked. "My life will be ruined if I have to go back to school."

"I'll look into it," Margo replied. "Now let's have something to eat."

Katie and Jonathon took the news reasonably well, never doubting their mother's experiences for a minute. They felt the honesty and integrity of the letter, and realized that they had some serious decisions to make as a family. The first decision that they all made was that they were not going to answer the phone, which rang off the hook all evening until they unplugged all of them from the wall. The second decision was that they would meet with the minister of their church. Margo had made an appointment with him for the next day after church. They decided not go to church, so as not to draw attention to themselves in public.

The four of them enjoyed each other's company all evening, eating, laughing, and playing games. They seemed to be bonding closer together. Whether it was the relief of finally having Matt back at home, or the unknown reaction that the public might have with Margo's televised testimony, the end result was togetherness. Taking a break from the phone and the television was also helpful to this reconnecting experience.

As Jonathon passed by the window in the family room, he noticed that a news truck was slowing moving down the street. He said, "Hey, Mom, Dad, is that one of the news trucks that you saw today?"

"What?" Margo and Matt asked simultaneously, running to the window.

"We've gotta get out of here," Matt said, grabbing their jackets.

"But, Matt, it's almost nine o'clock. Do you really think they'll come to the door?" Margo asked.

"Do you really want to take that chance?" Matt answered. "Let's go," he insisted. They piled into his truck and headed for his apartment. They figured that the media would be unable to find them for several days. There, they could figure out what to do next.

Chapter 6

Sal's Plans

Scientists seemed completely baffled as to the content of the materials on the Petersons's lot. They could not detect any known element in the metallic box foundation or in the clear cube. They could not understand why they could detect radioactivity in the ground, but not in the aboveground structures; and they could not explain or decode the strange writings on the cube. The mysterious cube began to draw national attention, and cars containing curious onlookers were lined up for several miles.

Reverend Sal made himself a cup of tea, and offered some to the Ellis family, but they declined. He invited them to have a seat, and asked to read a copy of the letter, which Margo had brought along in her purse. He read silently, nodding and occasionally raising his eyebrows. He sighed several times and finally looked up. "So you've all read this?" he asked.

"Yes," they responded.

"I'm curious to know what you all make of it," the reverend said. "Jonathon, would you please be first?"

"I think it's totally cool!" Jonathon answered. "I mean, it makes total sense that we're not the only beings in this humongous universe, and there's even a scientific explanation for 'rapture'!"

"Mm, hmm," the reverend responded, "and you, Katie?"

"Well, everything seemed so totally natural on Planet Peace, and yet they have knowledge of technology beyond ours. I think that's the part that makes me feel like it might be real because I think that's how God would want us to be: knowledgeable but natural," Katie answered.

"I see," said the reverend. "And you, Matt?"

"Well, I know my wife. She is a very reasonable and practical woman. And she had a very extraordinary experience. I know that I believe her. This letter, something rings true about it. I mean, it's almost like I know this Rebecca woman, and like I know that place. I can't really explain it," Matt said.

"And you, Margo?" Sal asked.

"Reverend, everything about this experience has seemed both *so real* and *surreal*. What I saw and heard out in that field was like no sound-and-light-show that I've ever seen. I don't believe that one exists like it anywhere in the world. The beauty of those two cubes, both the metallic and the clear, is unlike any artifact or piece of contemporary art that I've ever seen, and Matt and I have been to museums all over the world! But most of all, the words in that letter have touched me beyond all comprehension. Like Matt said, I feel as though I *know* Rebecca! I can't explain it either," Margo replied.

"Uh, huh," the reverend concluded. He thought for a while, with his chin in his hand, and finally looked up at each one of them. "I have to agree with each one of you. I have to say that I had the exact same thoughts as each one of you, with the exception of being present for the cube revealing. I know that you came here for answers. I don't have any. I know that you came here for guidance. I may be able to help with that. I can provide the counseling to help you determine your levels of faith, of love, and of charity. I can help to guide you through meditations. But before we go any further, I need to know one thing from all of you." He paused a long moment, and said, "Is there any doubt whatsoever in your mind that Planet Peace exists?" He paused again, and then asked, "Is this a hoax?"

Matt was the first to respond, "In my heart, Reverend, I have to say that the answer is 'No.'"

Katie was next, "Me, too."

Jonathon quickly added, "Me, too."

Margo said, "Reverend, I believe that Planet Peace exists. I believe that Rebecca is real, and that scientists figured out how to transport these exquisite boxes here. What I need to know from you is can you help my family to avoid an unspeakable existence here, in exchange for a merciful existence somewhere else?"

"*That*, my dear Margo, I believe I can do!" Sal answered.

They agreed to meet daily for instruction and guidance, and the family headed back to Matt's apartment, feeling like they had some direction. In the event that these cubes were a hoax, the worst thing that would happen would be that they would be taking up a lot of the reverend's time. But since he was willing and able to do so, it didn't seem to be a problem. If the clear cube was indeed a vehicle to a better place, they all agreed that they wanted to go. They began to wonder if they could bring other people. They also began to wonder who would be willing to go, and if they would be permitted to bring Franklin!

As they got closer to Matt's apartment, they could see television crews all set up in the parking lot. They had found out where Matt was staying! They turned around and headed back to church. Reverend Sal was surprised to see them. He was just locking up. When he heard that the media was stalking them, he invited them to stay in the church's shelter, which was currently vacant. He led them downstairs, and gave them all blankets and pillows for their cots, and showed them the food pantry, kitchen, and shower rooms. The Ellises were grateful for the meager accommodations. They were willing to stay here as long as it took for the media to turn their attention elsewhere.

The children were exhausted and fell asleep easily. Margo and Matt stayed awake, discussing their options over microwaved cups of hot cocoa. Margo expressed to Matt that she felt a deep sense of responsibility to share this information with as many people as possible, and yet, she did not want the children to be ridiculed or ostracized because of it. Matt indicated that the four of them were his primary concern, and that the children would have to decide for themselves whether or not they could withstand that kind of attention. He told Margo that she could create flyers, or newsletters, or even a Web site to educate people about Planet Peace. Margo loved the idea because it gave her a way to share the information anonymously, and then people could decide for themselves whether or not to attempt the teleportation process.

They picked up a newspaper on a table in the kitchen and read that a total solar eclipse was due to occur in three months, on August 21. There were solar eclipse clubs planning parties and events to celebrate the celestial occurrence. The article explained that total eclipses are rarer than partial eclipses, only occurring about once every eighteen years. Matt and Margo hoped that they would be able to learn how the clear cube would be activated via the solar eclipse, as the directions on the cube had mentioned.

The next morning, the Ellis family woke to the smell of eggs and bacon. Sal was preparing their breakfast, and mentally preparing their lessons. The family greeted him with big smiles, and gratefully indulged his kindness. Sal joined them with his own breakfast plate, and asked each one of them to render their definition of faith. Katie went first:

"Faith is what you believe in," she said.

Next, Jonathon offered, "Faith is *how much* you believe."

Matt followed with, "Faith is trusting that everything will be OK, no matter what."

Finally, Margo ended with, "Faith is believing in unseen and untold goodness, beyond all reason and doubt. It is trusting that God is the end result of everything."

Sal raised his eyebrows, "That was . . . very good. Perhaps you are all here to teach me!" Next, Sal asked each of his students to tell him about the time they felt the most loved.

Matt went first this time, "That's easy," he said, "when the kids were born."

Margo said, "Our wedding day."

Katie was next with, "My fifth birthday!"

Jonathon finished with, "Christmas!"

"OK, that's good, now I want you to close your eyes and remember how those days felt," Sal instructed. "Feel the feelings in your heart, and let them fill your head, your arms, hands, and all the way down to your feet. Hold those feelings." He watched as each one of them smiled and held their eyes closed. "Now, with your eyes still closed, try to increase the feeling some more, try to intensify the feeling, and realize that as much as you feel right now, God loves you thousand times more, so fill up with your love for him!"

"Wow," Matt said, "I could really feel that!"

"Yeah," Katie agreed, "that was really intense!"

"We're off to a good start," the reverend said. "Now, each of you, how can you be more helpful to your fellow man?"

"My folks are in a nursing home," Matt said, "they can always use more help around there."

"The city soup kitchens are always looking for help," Margo added.

"I can help with that," Katie offered.

"Me, too," Jonathon agreed.

"Well, then," Sal said, "meet you all here tomorrow morning to find out how it went!" He placed his dish in the sink and waved good-bye as he went up the stairs and out of the church.

The Ellis family sat around the table, with confused looks on their faces. This was Monday morning. They had not yet decided if Matt was going to work, or if the kids were going to school. Clearly, the reverend expected them to perform charitable acts today. Matt was the first to speak, "Well, I guess I'll stop at the nursing home after work."

"I'll look into home-schooling the children when we get back from the soup kitchen," Margo said.

"Yes!" the two young ones cheered. They cleared the table and got ready for their day.

Matt had an interesting day at the office. His coworkers and clients seemed more interested in his weekend than in their investments. By noon, he pushed everyone out of his office and was able to make a few phone calls. He was successful at doing business with his clients who lived at great distances. The local ones all seemed unavailable, or uninterested. He wondered how widespread the news had gotten about his wife's unusual experiences.

Margo and the children enjoyed working at the city soup kitchen. They focused themselves on service to the community and met a lot of caring and compassionate people. Some recognized Margo from the TV. They were genuinely interested in hearing about her experiences, and wanted to know more about the letter and the transportation device. Margo informed them that she was thinking of creating a Web site where she could post the letter and the transport instructions, as soon as she knew what they were. Some of the regular help at the soup kitchen gave Margo their e-mail addresses. She told the patrons who were interested to check the computers at the library for the Web site and promised to create it very soon.

Feeling exhausted, but deeply satisfied, the three drove back to the church to catch a small nap before dinner. Margo found Sal in his office when they returned, and she couldn't wait to share their experiences with him. Sal was pleased, particularly that the children were so eager to help.

Margo asked Sal if he could help her to establish a Web site where she could post information about this whole process. Sal agreed to help her in any way that he could, and the two began designing and setting up the Web site.

In the meantime, Matt left work and headed for the nursing home. He told the receptionist there that he was volunteering for the next few hours. She asked that he help out in the recreation room. He asked if he could visit with his parents briefly before the evening social activities began, and she informed him that it would be all right.

When Matt told his parents that he was volunteering this evening, they stared at him with disbelief. After a long pause, his mother asked, "Are you dying?"

"What? No, Mother, I am not dying!" Matt insisted.

"Are you doing community service for a crime you committed?" his father asked.

"No, Dad! I'm just here to be kind to my fellow man!" he shouted.

"Shh!" A nurse stepped into the room. "Please keep it down, we have people sleeping!" she said.

"Oh! Sorry!" Matt said.

"A real humanitarian!" his father snorted.

"Look, are you guys going to make fun of me all night, or what? How about coming down to the rec room and enjoying a game of bingo?!" Matt asked.

"You gotta be kidding me," Matt's father chuckled. "I wouldn't play bingo with those old hens if you paid me."

"Me, either," his mother added.

"Now wait a second, are you telling me that you never join in on the events downstairs?" Matt asked.

"Oh, we go when there's free food, but that's about it," Matt's mother answered.

"Well, you know what? I think that's sad. Let's get out of here. *Nurse*! I need two wheelchairs, please!" Matt requested.

"Matthew, stop it right now! I am *not* going down there!" Mrs. Ellis insisted.

"Oh, Mother, get in and be quiet," Matt retorted, lifting his mother from the bed to the chair.

"Now, son, don't think you're gonna do that to me!" Mr. Ellis warned.

"I'll be back for you in five minutes, Dad," Matt grinned.

Matt wheeled his parents into the elevator and into the recreation room. He began to distribute the bingo cards and refreshments. Two women wheeled up to the Ellises' table. One of them was named Vera, and she was almost blind. The other, Beatrice, was slightly paralyzed in her right hand. Matt's job was to help everyone with their bingo chips. He found himself having fun, enjoying the company of his parents, and of the ladies who had joined them.

Time flew by quickly. Matt distributed small prizes to the winners and assisted his parents up to their room after the game. "See? Now wasn't that fun?" he asked them.

"A ball! His father answered sarcastically.

"Oh, Henry, be quiet!" Mrs. Ellis joined in. "Matthew, it was delightful. Now, shouldn't you be getting back to your family?"

"Well, I thought I would help you guys out with your dinner trays," Matt said.

"No, dear, we'll be just fine. I'm very proud of you for helping tonight," Matt's mother said.

"Yeah, me too," Matt's father added. "Now get out of here before you eat all of my food!"

Matt drove back to the church, feeling profoundly changed by volunteering. He knew that his parents would be surprised, and rightly so. After all, he had spent most of his life only caring for himself and his immediate family. But now, things were different; he could feel it.

He drove by a park and saw some children playing there. He felt connected to them, and to their parents, and to all of the people that he had just met at the nursing home. He wondered how many of them would be taken by the "rapture," and how many would be left on Earth? He cringed to think of his parents, or any of the people that he had met this evening, being left on a destructive, worrying, burning planet. *Surely there was plenty of time. It couldn't be just around the corner, could it?* He turned on the car radio, and found that tensions in the Middle East had erupted into a full-blown war. Countries were scrambling for allies, weapons, and donations. But just a few feet away, children were playing in a park. He couldn't let it all end in devastation without trying to help people out. He determined to help Margo as much as he possibly could with her Web site, with newsletters, and flyers. He would try to reach as many people as he could with the news of this "rapture-like" transportation device.

Chapter 7

The Park

With the Web site well under way, and Matt on his way home, Margo decided that the family should eat dinner out this evening. They could remain relatively anonymous at a drive-through restaurant, and maybe pick up some clothes at the house afterward. The children woke up hungry, just as Matt was arriving back at the church. They all had a lot to share about their experiences.

They said goodnight to the reverend, who gave them a key to let themselves back in, and left for a fast-food restaurant. Everyone wanted to talk at once, so the parents allowed the children to speak first. Jonathon said," Dad, it was so cool! I mean, helping all those people! And they were really nice. They weren't freaks or anything!"

"Yeah," Katie agreed. "They were very nice. Every once in a while, somebody really smelled like alcohol or body odor, but mostly they were kind and grateful. It felt good to serve them food."

Margo glowed as she watched the children tell their father of their experiences. She told Matt about how some of the other workers had recognized her from TV and were very curious about the cubes and Rebecca's letter. She told Matt that she had assured them that she would be getting the information out to the community, and promised that they'd be the first to know. Matt was glad to hear that the Web site had been established, and wondered how the home-schooling was coming along.

"Sal and I took a break from the Web site, and I took the opportunity to check out home-schooling," Margo answered. "I sent for some curriculums, and I have a lot of paperwork to fill out and mail in, but it looks as though it will be easy enough."

"Great," Matt said. "Now let me tell you about my folks and their friends at the nursing home." Matt proceeded to tell his family of his adventures with all the bingo players and their antics. He shared that it was sad to see how disabled some of them were, and yet they persevered in having some fun, just for the sake of having some quality of life. It made him feel both happy and sad at the same time. He was glad to help as many people as he could with their bingo chips, their wheelchairs, their refreshments, and their prizes. He told them that his parents were doing well, that they were still mocking him, and that they wished Margo and the children well.

The Ellis family made it through the drive-through unnoticed and started toward their house to retrieve some clothing and supplies. Franklin was running out of dog food at the church shelter. When they arrived near their home, they did not see any vans, but there were some cars parked on the street with people sitting in them. They decided not to take any chances and drove around the corner to the street behind their house. Leaving Franklin in the car, they snuck between the houses to their back door, and keyed-in in the dark. They kept the lights off, as they each went to their rooms to retrieve clothes and miscellaneous items. Packing up some food from the kitchen, they left the house, unnoticed by anyone. When they got to the car, they all laughed hysterically, because they all felt like they had robbed their own house. Franklin had begun barking and jumping up and down when he saw everyone returning to the car. They shoved everything into the trunk and took off as fast as they could for the church, before anyone could spot them.

The smell of pancakes and waffles awakened the Ellis family on Tuesday morning, and Reverend Sal's smiling face greeted them yet again. "Well, how are my students this fine morning?" he asked.

"Happy! Glad to see you, as always, Reverend," Matt answered.

"Hungry!" Jonathon added.

"Sleepy," Katie joined in.

"Snow White, here. All present and accounted for," Margo joked.

"OK, then, enjoy your breakfast," Sal said. "I have some fun things in store for us today. Matt, can you take the day off from work?"

"Gladly!" Matt answered. "It will be nice not to be hounded today. I'll make my phone calls in the evening from here."

"Perfect!" Sal answered. "Eat up!"

The Ellis family was pleased to be treated with such great hospitality, and they were having fun getting to know Sal better. They told him of their adventures of the previous day, and he wholeheartedly enjoyed hearing about them. After they cleaned up, he said, "I'll meet you down at the church van in one hour. That should give you time to get showered and dressed."

Jonathon asked, "Can we bring Franklin?"

"Oh yes, he'll love where we're going," Sal answered.

When the Ellis family arrived at the church van, they found Sal putting picnic baskets and athletic equipment into the back of the van. "Hop in!" he said.

Sal drove to a state park, which was not at all crowded on a weekday morning. He parked the van and said, "We're going to play some games." The children took the baseball bats, gloves, and balls out of the car and immediately started playing with them. Sal called them back in for a prayer: "Lord, we bless this day, and this family. You have presented them with a challenge which is like no other that has come before. We thank you for your guidance and assurance as we walk this path, preparing ourselves to meet you some day, hoping that we all meet with your approval. We thank you for the lessons that you provide which strengthen us in faith, love, and charity, and we thank you for teaching us how to be quiet and still to connect with you in spirit. In the name of Jesus, we pray."

All answered, "Amen."

They tossed the baseballs back and forth to each other, as they tossed ideas about the Web site and flyers that they might distribute. They played until they were tired, and then Sal called them all together to stand in a circle. He said, "We're going to play the trust game. What is faith, but trust? We've got to start trusting each other if we are ever going to trust God. So, do you know how to play?" he asked. The kids shook their heads "No," as the parents uttered "Yes." Sal explained that each person would have a turn where they would fall backward in complete trust that the person behind them would catch them. "We've played catch with balls, now we're playing catch with people!" he said.

So they took turns catching each other, laughing, and making idle threats if anyone should drop someone. No one was hurt, and everyone agreed that they all felt more trusting of each other.

Sal was ready to change gears. "Now, let's have a seat, and imagine something," he said. "Close your eyes and imagine that you have just woke up in a strange place in the dark, and you get up and start running as fast as you can. You are running, and running, and you trip, and you fall. You are hurt, but you get up, and you keep running in the dark. Now you sense that either people or animals are running after you, and they are gaining on you, but you run faster. You trip again, and you are more hurt. But you get up, and keep going. They are gaining on you, it's pitch black, and you don't know where you are going, but you know that you have to get away, and suddenly, you are falling. You are in midair, in the dark, and falling. Now, all at once, I want you to recall the happiest memory that you have that we discussed yesterday. Feel the happiness, the joy, and the love. Let the love intensify, you are still falling, you are still in the dark, but you feel the deepest love that you have ever felt before in your life. And with eyes still closed, and still free-falling, and the love ever increasing, you realize that you know that you are going to be all right. No matter what happens, you realize that you trust that you will be fine. Everything will be OK. You have total, 100 percent faith in God, and the divine powers of the universe. And no matter what happens, everything will be in your best interest. Know that you are cared for and loved. You are cherished by your divine Creator, and all will be well." Sal watched the four peaceful, smiling faces and knew that he had achieved his goal. All four of them now knew faith a little bit better than they knew it before. "OK, come back to me," said the reverend. "How was that?"

"I had a little trouble going from fear to happiness, but I got it after a while," said Katie.

"Yes, it takes practice," responded the reverend, "and now you know how to do this exercise to increase your faith! Anyone else?" The other three were sitting on the ground, still stupefied from the meditation. "OK, well, we'll practice that some more another time. How about some lunch?" Once again, the Ellis family was glad to receive Sal's generous hospitality.

The family enjoyed the sandwiches and salads that Sal had made for them. It seemed he had thought of everything. While they were eating, he had also prepared the next lesson. Since Katie was the first one to finish, Sal took her aside, away from the other Ellises. "Katie, let's have a chat," he said, and turning toward the others, "excuse us, family, for a few minutes!"

The Ellis family watched as Sal took Katie over to another picnic table. They could not hear what was being said. "Katie," Sal asked, "have you ever lost, or almost lost something or someone that was very dear to you?" Katie thought for a moment.

"Yes!" she answered. "My mom had given me this ring," she showed him the ring on her left ring finger. It was a cobalt-blue sapphire in a triangle shape, set in an old-fashioned, embossed silver setting. "It was my grandmother's ring, and my mom had given it to me the day my best friend moved away. She thought it would cheer me up, and it did! One day, I looked down at my hand and the stone was missing! I immediately started crying and freaking out. I was alone in the house, and I was talking to myself and screaming "Oh my god! Where is it?'" I got on my hands and knees and touched every bit of the carpeting in the house, scoured the kitchen floor with my hands, and then every countertop and table. I remembered that I had done the laundry, so I even felt the bottom of the washing machine and the dryer! I still couldn't find it! I was crying so hard that I couldn't see, and I was really relying on my hands to find it. I was completely devastated, and my mom would have killed me if I had lost it!"

"What did you do?" Sal asked.

"Well, I went over the entire house again, with my hands, and I finally decided to look in this box of junk that I was throwing away, and there it was!" Katie answered. "Right there in the middle of a bunch of useless papers and trash! I picked it up and started kissing the dumb thing. I was so happy, that I started crying all over again!" Sal was listening intently.

"Mm, hmm, I see," he said. "Did you ever think, Katie, that that is exactly how God would feel if he ever lost you, and then found you again?" Katie looked shocked. She said, "I never thought of it that way!" Sal said," God loves every single one of us. We are all his precious gemstones, even when we are lying among trash and debris! He delights when we seek to connect with him. Think of how much he loves us, good qualities and bad, flaws and all. Really think about it. Then see if you can intensify your love for him in return."

"I will, Reverend," Katie said with tears in her eyes.

Sal motioned for Jonathon to come over to the picnic table next. When the boy sat down, he asked him, "Jon, have you ever lost something that was very dear to you?" Jonathon looked up at Sal, fighting the urge to cry.

"I lost the baseball championship for my team last summer," he said. "It was the worst thing that ever happened to me. I felt completely useless. Totally worthless. We had worked so hard that season. I couldn't even look at my friends after that. They called me, and came over to hang out, but I just stayed in the house. It was the worst summer ever."

"Mm, hmm, I see," Sal said. "How do you think God felt about you losing that championship?"

"I dunno, I mean, I never thought about it."

"Do you suppose that God was only happy for the winning team, and didn't care for you?"

"No," Jonathon said, looking like he was trying to figure out where the reverend was going with all of this.

"Where do you think God stands with teams and games and championships?"

"Well, I guess if we're all God's children, then he would wish that we *all* could win!" Jonathon surmised.

"Exactly!" the reverend exclaimed. "God loves us all equally, and unconditionally. Now, I have a few more questions for you. The loss of that championship might not have hurt so badly if you didn't love baseball so much, huh?" Jonathon nodded affirmatively.

"Do you think God loves baseball?" Sal asked. Jonathon started laughing.

"Yeah, I bet he does!"

"Does he love you, Jon?"

"Yes."

"Do you think he loves you more than baseball?" the reverend asked.

"Probably," Jon replied.

"I would bet that he does," Sal agreed. "So we have determined that while God loves baseball, he loves you and all of the players of baseball even more, and equally and unconditionally. Agreed?"

"Yes," Jonathon answered.

"Sometimes the love of something or someone can be disappointing, or it can hurt so bad that that you think that your life is ruined forever, but if we remember that God's love is always there, always present, and more powerful than any other thing in the universe, then we have nothing to fear or worry about. One more: do you know how many people there are on this planet?" Sal asked.

"Seven or eight billion, I think," Jonathon replied.

"How many of those people does God love?" inquired the reverend.

"All of them," answered Jon.

"That's pretty big, huh? Sal asked. Jonathon raised his eyebrows and answered, "Yeah, that's pretty big."

"OK, think about that. And send your mom over here, OK, Pal?" the reverend requested.

"Sure thing, Reverend," Jon said.

Margo wandered over as the kids took up another game of catch with their dad. She was very curious as to what was about to happen here, because both of her children returned to their table with wet eyes and smiles on their faces. Sal asked her to have a seat, and then asked her if she had ever lost anything dear to her. It took less than five seconds for Margo to mentally return to the neonatal intensive care unit when Katie was born.

"We almost lost Katie," she said. "It was the happiest time of our lives, and all of a sudden, it wasn't. The pregnancy had gone well, and the delivery, too, but when they went to check her Apgar score, she wasn't responding! She had breathed in some feces from the amniotic fluid into her lungs, and it had made her very sick. We instantly went from crying tears of joy, to tears of complete anguish. They were really having trouble reviving her. I never want to feel that kind of pain again."

"Can you imagine what it must be like for God to release us to the world from heaven?" Sal asked.

"What?" Margo asked, completely stunned at his question.

"I was just thinking that it must be difficult for God to create us all so uniquely, then to let us go to the Earth. He must be so completely delighted at our return," Sal explained.

"Yes, well, I'm sure, I mean, I never thought about it. But what does that have to do with Katie?"

"Don't you see? The level of joy and the level of pain you experienced with your firstborn all in the same day: it has to be a mere fraction of what God experiences as he creates us, releases us, and receives us home again."

"Wow, Reverend! That really opens up a whole new perspective on things! Where do you get this stuff?"

"You spend a lot of time thinking about God in my profession."

"Obviously. Well, is that it? Are you ready for Matt?"

"Yes, Margo, thank you."

"Oh no, Reverend, *thank you*!" Margo replied.

Matt handed his glove and ball to Margo as he made his way over to the picnic table with Sal. He was a little nervous, looking at his family's reactions as they returned to their picnic table. He was never very comfortable in analysis or therapy-type situations.

"Hello, Matt!" greeted Sal.

"Hello, Reverend."

"I'll make this quick, I can see that you are uncomfortable."

"Well, I just don't know what to expect, that's all."

"Just one question, Matt. Have you ever lost anything?"

"Ah, Reverend. You really know how to get a guy right here," Matt touched his fist to his heart. "Yeah, I almost lost my family, and recently, too."

"Oh, right. The separation. If this is too fresh to talk about, I'll understand."

"No, Reverend, it's OK. I really should talk about it. We'd have been a lot better off talking to you about it a long time ago, I'm guessing."

"OK, then."

"Well, I've been an idiot. I had everything a man could ever hope for, and I blew it. The best wife, the best kids, the best friends, house, car, and everything you can name. But the stress of life was getting to me, and I started yelling at my family, the way my old man used to. He's a grumpy old cuss. And that's exactly what I was becoming."

"And then?"

"Well, all of this happened. And it has given me another chance with my family. It has given me an opportunity to show my wife that I can be her best friend again, and a good father again. Weird as the whole thing may be, I'm actually grateful to just *be here* for everybody."

"Has God ever abandoned you?"

"Well, I guess there were times when I thought that he did. But every time I look back on one of those times, I can see it was just me not listening to him."

"Exactly. We're through. Let's go."

Chapter 8

Some "Doctoring"

Sal had instructed each member of the Ellis family to give a lot of thought to their private conversations with him, and then discuss it with each other at some point, preferably when they were all together. He began to head the van toward the city, as they all chatted about lighter topics. When Sal switched on the car radio, news of the war erupting in the Middle East was on every station. This was the first time that the children were aware of the situation, as Margo and Matt had not discussed it with them yet.

Sal turned off the radio when he noticed everyone's facial expressions turning fearful. He asked, "How does this new world development make you feel?"

"Afraid," Katie answered.

"Scared," Jonathon replied.

"Concerned," said Margo.

"Ditto," Matt concurred.

The reverend saw another teaching opportunity in this world event. "This is precisely when we need to be strong in our faith," he said. "Remember that being created in God's image and likeness means that we are cocreators with him. And nothing in this world is created by man unless it is preceded by thought. Thoughts precede action, therefore, what we *think* about this war can actually contribute to the outcome. Thoughts are prayers, and prayers are thoughts. Control your thoughts and prayers, and keep them focused on peace. *Trust* in positive outcomes. 'As a man thinketh, so he becomes.' 'If ye have faith but of a mustard seed, ye can say to that mountain "move," and it will do so.' The Bible is filled with suggestions for keeping thoughts positive, and now Rebecca has given us even more incentive to do so!"

The Ellis family agreed that their teacher was correct, and so they all took turns giving examples of pleasant outcomes to this global disturbance. The children imagined what reporters might say if the war suddenly ended and a peace treaty were signed. Margo and Matt took it a step further and imagined a worldwide effort at permanent peace that spanned from grassroots to the United Nations!

Sal said, "Now we're talking! This is exactly the kind of daydreaming and brainstorming that we've been talking about! It's the kind of thinking and praying that changes the world, one step at a time! I'm very proud of all of you. From now on, I think it is best if we stay focused on world peace, and avoid the deluge of media negativity." He pulled the van into a metered parking space, and the family stepped out into an abandoned lot. This was not the nicest section of Philadelphia, by any means. There wasn't a single car or building in their immediate surroundings that wasn't damaged or graffitied in some way. They saw a crowd of smiling people coming toward them on the sidewalk. Each one of them was carrying either gardening tools, or pots of trees and plants. There were even some children with their arms full of rubber gloves and trash bags. Sal greeted his friends with an equally big smile, and introduced the Ellises to his sister congregation. Today's lesson in charity would involve the cleanup, and transformation of this vacant lot into a beautiful park. The reverend and his four students happily put on some gloves and got to work.

The news regarding the war in the Middle East was so big and consuming of TV airtime that the story of the cube in the middle of a field in Bucks County, PA, fell by the wayside. As the attention came off Margo and her "missing family," the Ellises felt safe returning to their home briefly, after getting cleaned up at the church, to retrieve some more supplies, and to return the phone calls of worried relatives and friends. They had decided as a family to continue to stay at the church, and to not tell anyone of their whereabouts, but they agreed to phone everyone and to tell them that they were OK. The answering machine also had messages from the school regarding the children's absences. Margo called the school from her cell phone, and spoke to the principal. She was on good terms with this woman, and since Margo had often volunteered at the school, the principal had a lot of respect for her. What Margo didn't realize, or expect, was that the principal also had a lot of sympathy for her, and was relieved to hear that they were all right. When Margo informed Mrs. Demberg that she would be home-schooling the children, Mrs. Demberg was upset, but she understood. She told Margo that she would never receive all of the proper paperwork and curriculums back in time to finish the school year on schedule. She told Margo that if she could receive a doctor's note saying that the children had mononucleosis, or some other contagious disease, then she could have the final month's work sent home, and the children could finish school by mid-June with the rest of their classmates. Then they would be free to start the next school year whenever they wished. Margo thanked Mrs. Demberg for being so cooperative, and she apologized for the clandestine way they were living their lives. Mrs. Demberg assured her that if it had been anyone else, she would not have offered this kind of help. It was this level of respect that Mrs. Demberg had for Margo, which left her so curious about the cubes and the letter. "Margo," Mrs. Demberg asked, "I was wondering if I could have a copy of that letter you found in the cube."

"Actually, Mrs. D, I'll give you the Web site address where I have it posted. Feel free to share the address with anyone who wants it. Also, if anyone wants to communicate with me, they can e-mail me via that address."

"Thanks, Margo, I will. I wish you all the best, and I just want to let you know that there are a lot of people around here who believe you, and would stand by you, no matter what happens."

"Thanks, Mrs. D. You have no idea how much that means to me."

"You mean a lot to others. Please let me know if there is anything else that I can ever do for you."

"Just share the information. That's all I ask. Then, people can make their own decision about what to do."

They said good-bye, and hung up, after Margo promised to forward a note about the kids having mono. Matt was on the phone with a client, and the children were packing up some clothes and video games from their rooms. Franklin was running around the house, happily. He had clearly missed his familiar surroundings. They all did.

With the laundry finished, and the car fully loaded with duffle bags and sacks of groceries, the family set off for the church. Tonight, they decided, it would be *they* who would be the chefs. It was time for Sal to be the recipient of a home-cooked meal. Their muscles ached from the hard day of trash pickup, tilling, and gardening, but they each had a deep sense of satisfaction at making a dingy lot beautiful, and they looked forward to one more charitable act of feeding Sal.

They found him sitting at the computer in his office, his eyes wide and mouth hanging open. "Margo, you have got to see this!" Sal was referring to the Planet Peace Web site that they had created. It had already received over three hundred hits, after only being established for twenty-four hours!

"This is fantastic!" Margo squealed. She had 150 e-mails waiting for her. "Reverend, I'm gonna need a little bit of help."

"Right. I'll go get my laptop, and we'll get started."

"Kids, how about giving me a hand with dinner while these two get to work?" Matt asked.

Katie put a huge pot of water on the stove for pasta while Jonathon unpacked the groceries.

"Hey, Dad," Jonathon said," I've been doing some research on solar eclipses."

Matt was stocking the pantry. "Yeah? What have you learned?"

"Well, first of all, there are all types of eclipses, and several types of *solar* eclipses. A *total* solar eclipse is rarer than a partial, and only occurs about every eighteen years. That's why all these space nerds are making such a big deal out of it, planning parties and stuff. The next total solar eclipse will be on August 21."

"Oh yeah, your mother and I read about that in the paper. What else did you learn?"

"That the shadow space is called an 'umbra,' and that it can last for up to seven and a half minutes."

"Anything else?"

"Oh yeah, this is the coolest part. The free encyclopedia says that the word 'eclipse' comes from a Greek word that means 'I cease to exist.'"

"That's, uh . . ." Matt was at a loss for words.

"That's just creepy, if you ask me," Katie said.

"OK, let's just get back to making dinner," Matt said.

The Petersons's lot was no longer drawing the amount of attention that it had drawn the previous weekend. The police had closed the case on the vandalism idea, and some NASA specialists were flying up from Florida to examine the materials that the cubes and the letter were made of. Occasional onlookers would drive up and take pictures, and read the inscription on the clear cube. They'd make some jokes about this being a great site for a "Mothership Airport," which is what the tabloids were reporting that it was, and when they would run out of things to joke about, they'd get in their cars and drive away. The Petersons's were instructed to hold off on the construction of their new home until the NASA specialists could make some determination about the cubes.

Phil Peterson was complaining to his current neighbor about the whole thing. "I just don't see where these officials think they can just tell me what I can and can't do. Who do they think they are, anyway?" Dr. Curtis Lasky listened to his neighbor with halfhearted sympathy.

"Well, Phil, I'm sure that it's all about public safety . . ."

"Safety? I'll give them safety, right between the eyes!" Phil interrupted. "These clowns don't know what we've been through. We saved all of our lives for that property, and for the retirement of our dreams. And now we've got to wait and see if we can get this godforsaken lawn ornament out of there before we can go on with our lives! I have mind to take a stick of dynamite over there and blast the thing to kingdom come! Then it will really be a 'vehicle to a distant land.'"

Dr. Lasky had listened to Phil rant and rave about one thing or another for years. He was secretly elated that the Petersons were finally moving. He knew the Ellis family from church, and took pity on Margo when he learned that Phil was furious with her. He wished that he could see her again to tell her so and hoped that the missing family was all right. "Have you heard anything about the missing family?" Lasky asked.

"No, but I hope they're all *dead*! That stupid woman brought me nothing but trouble. If I ever see her again I'll choke her, and her little dog, too!"

Curtis had a vision of Phil Peterson turning into the "Wicked Witch" from the *Wizard of Oz* movie, and couldn't help but hear the chasing music from the movie in his head. He wondered if anyone from the church had heard from the family. He decided that he would stop over there later, and have a talk with the reverend about reaching out to the missing family somehow. Sal and Margo managed to respond to all of the e-mails just in time for dinner. Matt and the children had prepared spaghetti and meatballs, with salad and garlic bread, and everyone sat down to enjoy it. They blessed the food, and began eating. Margo remarked that she must be the luckiest woman in America, because she couldn't remember the last time she had cooked a meal! They laughed and joked and entertained each other with stories of meatball mishaps and spaghetti food fights. Jonathon shared his new knowledge of solar eclipses, and all were eerily impressed of its ancient Greek meaning.

"It didn't just translate as 'I cease to exist,' it also translated as 'I am absent."'

"Well, you are, as a matter of fact," Margo responded. "And I spoke to your principal about it today. She says I just need to get a note from a doctor saying that you both have mono, and they'll send your work home for the remainder of the year."

"Wow," Matt said. "That's awfully nice of her. Where are we gonna get a thing like that?"

"I don't know, but I'll think about it tomorrow. I'm too exhausted to think about it tonight," Margo answered.

"Hey, we should talk about our one-on-ones with Sal," Katie suggested.

"OK by me, you all right with it, hon?" asked Matt.

"Sure. Go ahead Katie."

"Well, the reverend asked me if I ever lost anything, and I told him the story about my ring. He said that we are all like precious gems to God, and if he ever lost one of us, he would be devastated."

"That's pretty profound. Anything else?" Matt asked.

"Yeah, he said that he would be totally happy if we were ever found."

"I get it. How about you, Jon?"

"Reverend asked me the same question. I told him about last year's baseball championship."

"Do you remember what we talked about, Jon?" Sal asked.

"Yes. You said that while God loves baseball, he loves the players more. And we should never get so upset over stuff that we love, because God's love is bigger than everything."

"Excellent. You are great students!" the reverend exclaimed.

"I was next," Margo said. "The reverend asked me the same question. I told him about the day Katie was born. He reminded me that as much joy as we felt when she arrived, and as much pain as we felt when we thought we almost lost her, God's joy and pain must be greater. After all, he makes us, and then he sends us to the earth. He waits a long time to see most of us again."

"Mine was simple," Matt said. "I told him that I've been a real jerk, and now I have a second chance to be with all of you. He asked if God ever left me, and I told him 'No,' that he never had. I only thought that he had, whenever I wasn't listening to his clues."

"Excellent! Excellent! You guys are the best! You really pay attention, and you are doing well with all of your lessons. By the way thanks again for helping with the lot transformation today. You all worked very hard, and I know that a lot of people appreciate it."

Just then, they heard some rapping on the door upstairs. The reverend excused himself, and went to see who had come to the church at such a late hour. He was surprised to see Curtis Lasky standing there with a bag of groceries.

"Hello, Curtis! What brings you here this evening?"

"Hi, Reverend. I just wanted to bring this contribution to the church shelter. Also, I was wondering if anyone has heard anything from that family who's been missing."

"Why do you ask?"

"I was just wondering. My neighbor is Phil Peterson: the guy whose property that cube is on. He's still going on about the whole thing, and I was just feeling sorry for that family. Has anyone heard from them?"

"Listen, I've got something on the stove downstairs. Can you wait here a minute?"

"Sure, Reverend."

Sal took the bag of groceries downstairs and told the Ellis family of Curtis's arrival. "You realize, Margo, that he is a physician," Sal said.

"No, Reverend, I didn't realize that."

"Shall we ask him the favor of writing that note?"

"Oh, Sal, I would really hate to impose on him like that. Besides, it doesn't seem right."

"It seems to me like a gift! A very timely one at that!"

"Well, we don't even know if he'd be willing to do something like that. I mean, risking his reputation and all," Matt offered.

"All we can do is ask, but he seems extremely sympathetic to your cause!" Sal responded. "And Phil Peterson is his neighbor!"

"Oh god! No! We can't risk him saying anything to Phil!" Margo whispered loudly.

"Margo, I assure you that he will not say anything to Phil. I gather that he is not his favorite person," Sal responded.

"Well, we could give it a shot," Matt said. "What do you think kids? We haven't told a soul where we are, and you guys have been great at keeping a secret. Should we ask this doc for a note?"

"I guess," Jon offered.

"Sure, why not?" Katie said.

"How shall we do this?" Sal asked.

"Let's go upstairs," Margo said.

The Ellis family went upstairs, following Sal. "Curtis, I really want to thank you for those groceries," he said as he rose up the stairs. "And there's something I'd like you to see . . ."

Curtis's eyes were wide with surprise, and he greeted the family with hugs and smiles, relieved that they were all right. "Wow, I'm glad to know that you guys are OK," he said. "Have you been here the whole time?"

"Yes. Sal has been very kind," Margo answered.

"Of course. I don't blame you. I think I would have done the same thing. Hey, Matt! It's good to see you, man. You haven't been around for a while."

"Yeah, Curtis. We actually were separated for a while," Matt answered.

"Oh, I'm sorry. I didn't mean to pry."

"No, it's OK. Everything's fine now."

"Glad to hear it. I'm divorced myself. Miss my family terribly. It's great you guys were able to work it out."

"Hey, Curtis, you hungry?" Jonathon asked.

"That's 'Dr. Lasky,'" Margo corrected.

"No, please, call me Curtis. And yes, actually, I am hungry. Something smells good here."

"Come on downstairs, my friend. There's plenty for everyone," Sal said, escorting everyone down to the shelter.

The family told Curtis everything, from the beginning. They all took turns, telling their sides of the story as it unfolded. From Margo's fateful walk with Franklin, to Matt coming back into their lives, to the kids missing school and all of the lessons with Sal. Curtis was now an official confidant. "You guys have been through a lot in five days!" he said. "What's the plan, now?"

"Well, we'll keep taking lessons with Sal," Matt answered.

"And we'll keep updating the Web site, and answering e-mails," Margo said.

"And we're going to create flyers and maybe a newsletter," Katie offered.

"And there's a solar eclipse coming in August that will tell us how to fly that box!" Jonathon exclaimed.

"Wow!" Curtis exclaimed. "That doesn't seem to leave much time for work or school!" The family remained silent, looking at each other.

"Matt has been able to get some work done, and Margo needs to move some of her files from home to here. But you bring up an interesting point, Curtis . . ." Reverend Sal explained. He told Curtis of the home-schooling dilemma, and of the courtesy of the school principal. He asked him if he'd be willing to write them a note.

"Look, I'd like to help you folks out any way that I can, but this is sort of compromising," Curtis seemed embarrassed.

Margo immediately responded with, "We completely understand. It's an imposition and we don't want—"

Sal interrupted with, "Curtis, there would be no trouble. Mrs. Demberg is completely sympathetic."

"Look, we can't make the Doc do anything he doesn't want to do, so let's just finish up our dinner and call it a night. It was great seeing you again, Curtis. I hope we see you again soon," Matt said.

"No hard feelings, man?" Curtis asked.

"Of course, not! Have a good night," Matt shook hands with Lasky.

Dr. Lasky had trouble sleeping that night. *That poor family!* He didn't know why he felt so attached to them. After all, he only knew them from church on Sundays! But they seemed so *nice*. He had seen Margo's testimony on the news, and it left him with a strange feeling. Here was someone that he greatly admired, and he felt her to be very reasonable and sensible. It must have all happened exactly as she reported, but there must be some logical explanation for that box being so deeply embedded in the ground almost overnight. And there must be another good explanation for the sound-and-light show that accompanied the exterior walls sinking into the foundation. And surely the letter was a hoax. But the family and the reverend all seemed quite sure that it was authentic! He rolled over and tried to get some sleep.

Chapter 9

Friends Telling Friends

Candy and Mike were missing their neighbors, the Ellises. They knew why they were staying away from their home, and they didn't blame them. Occasionally, a car would pull up in front of their house, and someone would sit there for hours. Mike had gotten home late from work on Tuesday night, and found his family asleep. He woke up early on Wednesday, and he had the day off. He decided to cut the Ellises' grass, and he was just finishing up, when he found Candy watering Margo's flowers. "Have you heard from Margo?" he asked her.

"She finally returned my call yesterday, I was worried sick!"

"What did she say?"

"She said that they're all right, but she won't say where they're staying. She gave me a Web site, and told me to try and reach her there."

"What are the kids doing about school?"

"She's home-schooling."

"Oh. Is Matt still working?"

"Yes. Since his clients are mostly at a distance, most of them don't know about their involvement in this cube thing."

"Maybe I'll try to meet him for lunch."

"I don't think they want to see anybody, Mike."

"I know my friend. He won't throw me out if I bring him an Italian hoagie."

"Suit yourself."

This time it was crepes. It seemed that there was no end to Sal's culinary abilities.

"Reverend, you've really got to stop spoiling us like this!" Margo said.

Katie wandered into the kitchen, rubbing her eyes. "Crepes!" she said. "I *love* crepes!"

"With strawberries and whipped cream!" Jonathon shouted.

"What's all the yelling about?" Matt asked. "Whoa, what's this? Are you serious? Is this a church shelter or The Four Seasons?"

"Oh, you all flatter me," Sal complained. "I just love cooking, that's all. And you have all given me a great excuse to indulge my favorite hobby!"

"My new favorite hobby is *eating*!" Jon exclaimed. They all laughed, and set the table for another exemplary breakfast.

"Well, family, what shall we do today?" Sal asked.

"Honestly, Reverend, I really should go to the office," Matt said.

"I need to catch up on some work, too," Margo said.

"Fair enough," Sal said. I have some parishioners that are in the hospital that I need to visit.

"What will we do?" Katie asked.

"You're coming with me," her mother said.

"Let's meet back here for dinner at six o'clock. I'll have dinner ready, and maybe some new lessons, too," Sal said.

"Sounds good, Sal," Matt said. "See you all tonight. Luv ya," he said, kissing the tops of their heads.

Margo cleaned up the kitchen, while the children showered and dressed. She was just about to get ready herself, when Sal came running down the stairs.

"How's strep throat or chicken pox?" he asked hurriedly.

"What?" Margo asked.

"Dr. Lasky has two patients who have strep throat and chicken pox. He has the ability to bring the infection to the children!"

"Wow! He really has a thing against lying! That's a good thing, though, isn't it? I suppose you think this is another godsend?"

"Well, now that you mention it . . ."

"Actually, the children have never had the chicken pox, and we always wanted them to get them. There's a school of thought that says they'll be healthier adults if they get a good case of it. Matt and I both had it. Have you?"

"Yes, I did. Listen, Margo, he's on the phone. Shall I tell him 'yes' to the pox?" the reverend asked.

"Let me call Matt and ask him first, then I'll call Curtis back."

"I'll get his number."

Matt agreed that this would be a good time for the kids to get the chicken pox. They had some friends who actually hosted some chicken pox parties, so that all the neighborhood kids could catch them. This seemed like a good time because they were sort of quarantined in the church basement anyway, and Margo was willing to stay in and take care of them, as long as she could bring all of her work from home to the church. Matt learned that the kids were not very excited about becoming infected, but they trusted their parents' judgments about health issues.

Matt managed to get lots of work done without his colleagues bothering him. They had run out of questions to ask him, and of ways to make fun of his predicament. At lunchtime, Matt looked up to see his neighbor at the door of his office. Mike was standing there with two large Italian hoagies. He didn't know which of them he was happier to see! They took the hoagies and root beers to a park across the street, and Matt filled Mike in on everything except where they were staying.

"That's pretty intense," Mike said. "How long are you going to keep this lifestyle up?"

"You mean living away from home? Probably until the wolves back off."

"What about these 'lessons?'"

"What d'ya mean? They're important to us."

"So, you mean you are actually going to try to go through with this? I mean, you're going to practice increasing in these three 'qualities' and meditation, and then try to activate this 'device' into the future?"

"You make it sound so foolhardy."

"Isn't it? I'm sorry, Matt, but *isn't it*?"

"Look, I can't explain why I know this is real. I just know. And isn't there a new war going on that has the potential to be World War III? And aren't scientists discovering more than a double helix of DNA when they look down the microscope? Isn't there a major energy crisis right now? Maybe I am a fool, but I know one thing: With my family is where I need to be. We're closer now than we've ever been. These lessons are changing us. We are all becoming better people. And if we stand around a clear cube in the middle of a field in the middle of the night one night, and we end up making a damn bunch of fools out of ourselves, well, then at least we're a *family* of fools. And I wouldn't have it any other way!"

"I'm sorry, man. You're right, I'm sorry. I had no right to judge you like that. I guess I just didn't want to believe that it's *this big*!"

"No hard feelings, man. Listen, check out the Web site. Jonathon's got some info on there about solar eclipses, and Katie's gonna help us to start making flyers and newsletters."

"Hey, maybe we can help you with the flyers and the newsletters!"

"You'd do that? You guys are the *best*!" Matt said, slapping his friend on the back.

"You know it! Who else would cut your damn grass on his day off?"

Margo and the kids arrived at their home to find Margo's sister, Vickie, sitting in her car, which was parked in front of the house. They walked up to her car, and Margo asked, "What are you doing here?"

"Oh my god! You scared me half to death!" Vickie said. "I was missing you guys, and hoping that you might show up here. How are you, munchkins?"

"Good, Aunt Vickie, we missed you too," Katie said.

"Guess what! We're gonna get the chicken pox!" Jon said.

"What? How do you know a thing like that?" Vickie asked.

"A doctor from our church is going to bring it to them, so they have a good excuse to stay out of school until the end of the year."

"Couldn't he just write you a note?"

"Too honest."

"Oh. Is he married?"

"As a matter of fact he's divorced. Come on inside. It looks like the media finally found something better to do than bug us today."

They went into the house. The kids took Franklin into the basement to play, while Margo filled Vickie in on everything except where they were staying.

"Sounds boring. So how did this doctor find you?"

"We bumped into him. He's meeting us at church later to infect the kids."

"That sounds so weird."

"This whole thing is weird."

"So you finally admit it! Are you ready to drop this whole thing, and go back to living a normal life?"

"Vickie, haven't you seen the news? What's happening now is just the tip of the iceberg! The energy crisis, the extra DNA strands, the war: it's all happening now! We're not sticking around to see how it all turns out if we have a chance to get out of here!"

"You guys are like some kind of cult. What are you gonna do if it doesn't work?"

"Then at least we tried!"

"And what if we never see you again?"

"That would be your choice. Everyone will have to choose. Here, I wrote the Web site down for you," Margo gave Vickie a piece of paper.

"What exactly do you want me to do with this?"

"Share it with everyone you know. They can contact me directly through that site."

"Mom's a nervous wreck. You should call her a little more often."

"I will. Thanks for coming over today, Vickie."

"I miss the kids. Can I see you guys again?"

"They'll have the chicken pox. Maybe you can help Katie to distribute her flyers for the Web site."

"Oh yeah, that's just what I want to do," Vickie said sarcastically. "I'll think about it."

"Hello, Jodi? This is Abby. Have you heard from Margo? She's not returning my calls," Abby said.

"Oh, hi, Abby. Yeah, she returned my call yesterday. She told me to call you and tell you that she's all right, but I forgot. Sorry."

"Did she say where they are, or how everybody is doing?"

"Apparently they're all fine, but they're not telling anyone where they're staying. The media have been staking out their house, and they're waiting for them to go away, before they come back home."

"Oh. They must be miserable!"

"No, they're really fine. In fact, Matt and she have reconciled, and they are all getting along great."

"Well, I guess that's what happens in a time of crisis. I just hope that they find the Lord."

"Margo claims to have found him years ago, Abby. Just not the way you find him."

"Is there any way that I can contact her?"

"Yes, she gave me this Web site. She said you can e-mail her there."

Jodi gave Abby the Web address, and then signed off with Abby. She logged onto the address herself, and then proceeded to call all of their mutual friends and acquaintances to tell them to do the same. Coincidentally, Abby did the same thing.

When Mike came home, he found Candy on the phone with his sister, Barbara.

"Barb wants to know if you saw Matt today," she asked.

"Yes. He sends his love," Mike answered.

"She wants to know if they're all right."

"Yes. They're actually doing really well. They're back together and everything."

"She wants to know why Margo's not returning her calls."

"Tell her to check out the Web site."

"Mike says you should check out the Web site. I told you to contact her that way. She told me the same thing. I know this all sounds crazy, but she did sound very happy and she sounded as sane as ever."

Candy hung up with Barbara, and Mike filled her in on his visit with Matt. He told her that he had volunteered them to help out with the flyers and newsletters. Candy was not very thrilled with the idea. She decided to log onto the Web site, and then she proceeded to call all her friends and give them the web address. Mrs. Demberg, Vickie, and Barbara had all done the same thing.

Chapter 10

A Friend in Need

Curtis knocked on the church side door, and Margo answered it quickly.

"Listen, Margo, I'm sorry about being so insistent on the children actually being sick . . ."

"No, it's OK, Curtis. I really appreciate your honesty and integrity. It's rare, nowadays."

"So, if the children are around, I can expose them to this culture," he pointed to his black bag.

"Sure. They're ready for you. Complaining, but ready, I think."

"You know, it's uncomfortable, but the real burden is going to be on you, taking care of them."

"No big deal. I'm ready. I've got my oven mitts for their hands so they don't scratch, and my calamine lotion and my oatmeal bath."

"OK, then. Let's do this. I'll get a note to Mrs. Demberg in the morning."

"Thanks so much, Curtis. We really appreciate you doing this."

Katie and Jonathon were playing video games and talking to their friends on their cell phones. They groaned when the saw Dr. Lasky come into the room.

"Now, be brave. It'll all be over in four weeks, and your body will be that much healthier for it," Margo assured the children.

"Hey, Mom," Katie said, "Is it OK if we tell our friends about the Web site?"

"I don't see why not, as long as they don't clutter the e-mails. They've tripled already!"

"Since when?" Curtis asked.

"Since Monday night."

"That's only forty-eight hours!"

"I know, isn't it great?"

"Margo, you're going to need some help!"

"Are you offering?"

"Um, well, I . . ."

"That's OK, I'm sure you're very busy."

"I can use some help with the flyers and newsletters!" Katie piped up.

"Katie!" her mother admonished.

"Give me some time to think about all of this, OK, Margo?"

"Sure, Curtis, take all the time you need. Like I said, I don't want to impose. But anything you could do would sure be helpful."

Curtis swabbed the children's arms with some of the culture from his bag. He told them that there is a fourteen-day incubation period before they will begin to see symptoms, and that it might take an additional seven to fourteen days for their symptoms to subside. Curtis assured Margo that he would let her know very soon whether or not he would be helping out with the "Planet Peace" Web site. She gave him the web address, and he promised to look it over as soon as he got home.

The Web site was receiving continuous hits. Almost everyone who looked at it sent an e-mail to it. Some of them were Margo's friends, wishing her well. But most of them were curious about the cubes, the letter, and this peaceful planet that had no fear. Margo decided to add a chat room to the Web site. She felt that it would be healthy for people to vent their fears and frustrations, as well as to share their curiosity. Now, more than ever, it was important that they did not feel alone. Like-minded people could connect and encourage each other to develop in the three qualities. Maybe they would even gather to practice group meditations!

When Sal arrived back at the church, he was pleased to learn that the hits on the Web site had tripled, and that the children had received their dose of chicken pox. "In honor of your new disease, tonight's entrée will be 'Chicken a la King', or in this case, 'Chicken a la Prince and Princess,' with a side of couscous, dotted with diced roasted red peppers to commemorate your spots!"

"Very funny, Reverend," Jonathon said.

"Yeah. What are you, a minister, a chef, or a comedian?" Katie quipped.

"Sal, you really should open up your own restaurant," Margo added.

"I think my boss has bigger things in store for me," Sal answered.

"What do you mean?" Margo asked.

"Margo, have you read some of these e-mails that people are sending in? These people are completely lost and desperate. They are loaded with fear and have absolutely no idea where to begin to correct their thinking. I think we need to post some of our lessons on the site."

"That's a great idea!" Margo exclaimed.

"And I've been thinking of offering a course here, or some type of seminar, where people can learn how to increase their faith, love, and charity skills."

"You could feed them, too!" Jonathon added comically.

"Yeah, Reverend. If you feed them, they will come," Katie said.

"Very funny," Sal said, "But the idea does have merit . . ."

Matt found himself driving home instead of to the church. His body was on "automatic pilot," and it seemed to always know the way home after work. He sat in his car in front of his house, thinking about what Mike had said, wondering if his friend was right. *Was this all just a giant hoax? Were they the victims of the biggest scam that ever hit Bucks County? Or was this as real as he believed it to be. The eclipse was two and a half months away. How much longer would it take before they were ready?* He was too tired to think of it. But Matt knew one thing for sure: each day that he worked on the three qualities, he was becoming less like his father, and more like the man that he knew himself to be. He realized that he felt more at peace now than he had ever felt in his life. He decided to trust in the process and let it unfold as it would. He headed toward the church, and passing the clear cube in the middle of the Petersons's property, he gave it a wink, and drove on.

At the dinner table, the kids filled everyone in on all the school gossip that they had learned, Matt filled everyone in on all the neighborhood gossip that he had learned, and Margo caught everyone up on family matters that she had learned from Vickie.

"How about you, Sal? How are the patients you visited today?" Matt asked.

"Oh, they're healing. But I'm afraid that their home is in great disrepair. The husband fell through the ceiling trying to repair the attic fan, and the wife had fallen on some broken tiles in the bathroom. This is an elderly couple with a low income. Are you off on Friday for the Memorial Day weekend?"

"Yes. Would you like some help fixing their place up?" Matt asked.

"I would greatly appreciate it," Sal answered.

"Count me in, Sal. I'll see if I can round up a few helpers as well."

"Nothing like a healthy dose of altruism on a long holiday weekend!"

On Thursday morning, NASA specialists met up with some scientists from Washington, DC at Philadelphia International Airport. They rented a ten-passenger van, loaded their equipment, and drove to Ottsville, PA. After checking into their hotel, they drove to the Petersons's lot and got to work. The metals and clear materials which made up the cubes proved to be unidentifiable. They notified their superiors of their findings and were given the authority to raise a protective fence. Local contractors were brought in to erect the fence, and "No Trespassing" signs were posted every few feet. Margo learned about the fence by checking in on the chat room.

Cubecutie: "Hey, have you seen these NASA guys putting a fence up all around the cubes?"

Margo: "No. What's happening?"

Cubecutie: "I don't know. All I know is that the police took the crime scene tape down, and now these nerdy types brought in a fence company and are hanging 'keep out' signs."

Margo: "Hmm, I wonder what that's about. Let me know if you learn anything new."

Cubecutie: "Sure Margo, anything I can do to help."

CuriousCurtis: "Margo, is that you?"

Margo: "Yeah, Doc, is that you?"

CuriousCurtis: "Yes, it's me. I just got through reading Rebecca's letter. I can see now why you feel that there's truth to all of this. Between your experience and this letter, it's all very compelling!"

Margo: "I know. So does this mean you'll help us?"
CuriousCurtis: "Yes. I think I'm ready to help you. At least then maybe I can get some sleep."
Margo: "Huh?"
CuriousCurtis: "Living alone has caused me to lie awake worrying about a lot of things. Lately, it has been you and your family."
Margo: "We are grateful to you, Curtis. See you tonight?"
CuriousCurtis: "Absolutely! What's for dinner?"
Margo: "Spot Fish and mixed vegetables. We also have a white iced cake decorated with Red Hots candies!"
CuriousCurtis: "Sounds like the chef has a 'sick' sense of humor."
Margo: "You have *no* idea! See you later!"

Margo signed off. She had promised Sal that she would stop at the grocery store and pick up the ingredients for tonight's dinner. It was a windy day, and Margo wanted to remain incognito, so she wrapped a scarf around her head, put on a large pair of sunglasses, and headed for the store.

Fumbling with her keys and her wallet, Margo was not watching where she was going, and walked straight into Jodi at the shopping cart stall.
"Margo?" Jodi asked.
"Oh! You're a sight for sore eyes! How are you?" Margo asked.
"I'm fine. The question is, how are you? You look like something out of a James Bond movie!"
"Well, I'm trying to not be noticed."
"It almost worked, until you were as subtle as a bull in a china store!"
"Sorry about that."
"No damage. Let's go inside. I'll help you get what you need and you can get out of here."

Margo had managed to get the few items on her grocery list and made it to the checkout counter in a matter of minutes. Just then, a woman recognized her.
"You're that woman on the news who has the Web site!" she said.
"What? No. I don't know what you're talking ab . . ." Margo stammered.

"No, she's not. Let's get moving, Ursula," Jodi said, using the nickname that she gave Margo in college.

"Yes you are! It's you! Well, I'm glad that I ran into you because I have something to say to you! I think that it's an absolute disgrace that you are perpetuating these lies in a public forum! There is only one word and one way, and that is the Bible! And there's nothing in there about a ride to heaven in a box! In Thessalonians, chapter 4, it says that we 'will be caught up with them in the clouds to meet the Lord in the air.'"

"Did it ever occur to you that that could just be a parable?" Jodi retorted. "Maybe this is one of the actual mechanisms of '*rapture*'!"

"How dare you even speak of it!" the woman answered. "You both should be ashamed of yourselves."

"Judge not, lest ye be judged," Margo countered, as Jodi shoved her out into the store foyer. "Thanks for being my body guard today."

"Just go back into hiding, will you? Otherwise I'm gonna have to dust off my brass knuckles and billy club!" Jodi joked.

"Do you *believe* that woman? I wonder if she belongs to Abby's church."

"Has Abby contacted you?"

"Yeah. She entered the chat room as 'Reborn Roomy.' But she wasn't all fire and brimstone like that lady."

"Listen, go back to your hole in the wall before somebody follows you, and enjoy your chicken pox fish."

"Spot fish."

"Whatever. I'll talk to you soon."

Chapter 11

Spot Fish Dinner

Katie and Jonathon found themselves bored and stuck at the church because of their contagious disease. They created a very simple flyer stating the Planet Peace Web site address, set on a faded background picture of Earth. They felt that the title of the Web site alone was enough to intrigue and interest people into having a look at it. As the printer began printing the flyers, they decided to snoop around the kitchen and the pantry to figure out what Sal had planned for dinner. They found the white iced cake in the microwave. When they lifted it out, they saw that it was covered in Red Hots candies. They began laughing and conspiring about ways to get back at the reverend with some kind of prank. Jon thought it would be fun to hide his weekly sermon book, or the collection baskets. Katie said that those pranks were too simple and obvious. She suggested that they call him to the hospital to do last rites on somebody. Her brother convinced her that that was too serious. They decided that they didn't know enough about him, and that they should ask him about his life for a change tonight at dinner.

Margo arrived home with the groceries and solved the mystery for the children by having them put the spot fish into the refrigerator.

"Oh, spot fish," they both said in unison.

"Yes, spot fish, my soon-to-be-spotted friends!" Sal announced, as he entered the room.

"Oh, hi, Reverend," Margo greeted him.

"Hello, Margo. I trust you had an uneventful trip to the grocery store."

"Well, actually, there was an altercation."

"You're kidding! What happened?"

"Some lady accosted me with her Bible."

"She hit you?" Jonathon asked.

"No, but she might as well have," Margo answered. "She told me that I should be ashamed of myself for promoting Rebecca's letter in a public forum."

"And are you ashamed?" Sal asked.

"No. I don't know. Maybe. No, I don't think so," Margo answered.

"How did you answer her?" Sal inquired.

"I told her that she should not judge me, lest she be judged herself."

"Excellent! You make me very proud of you. There is no telling if this is a hoax or if this is part of God's plan, but in either case, there is no need for judgment. He gives us all the will and discernment to make up our own minds."

"Well, there certainly are a lot of people who are moved enough by Rebecca's letter to believe it. There's a group that are protesting the fence around the cubes. Some of them even made signs!"

"Let's hope they're working on improving their qualities just as much as they are fighting to free the cubes!" Sal said, beginning to prepare the dinner.

"Free the Cubes!" Curtis shouted, as he entered the room holding Jon like a protest sign. Everyone laughed and greeted Curtis. Sal was pleased that he was joining them for dinner again.

"Just curious, Curtis, are you taking off tomorrow for the holiday weekend?" Sal asked.

"Yes, Reverend, did you have something in mind?"

"Two of our parishioners have a home in need of repair. Matt's helping, and hoping to round up some friends. Can we count you in?"

"Sure. My wife's taking the kids to see her family out west. If I stay home, I'll end up at the Petersons's barbecue. Fixing up somebody's broken home is definitely a better offer!" Curtis answered.

"Great! Since you're available for the whole weekend, then you can join us on Saturday for my big surprise!"

"What surprise?" the kids asked together.

"Another surprise?" Margo asked.

"What's this about a surprise?" Matt asked, as he entered the kitchen. He was greeted by hugs from the children and kisses from Franklin, who leaped into his arms.

"Welcome home, Matt. I was just about to tell the family that I have some amusement park tickets, and I'd like to take all of you on Saturday!" the reverend said.

"Sounds good. What did we do to deserve this?"

"Well, you're good parishioners, great students, and fantastic houseguests! Plus, you're going to help me repair a very broken house tomorrow!"

"With my help," Curtis added.

"And my neighbor, Mike," Matt added.

"The more, the merrier," said Sal," but I only have six park tickets."

"Oh, Mike won't expect a park ticket. He works for hoagies!" Matt explained.

"Speaking of food, dinner's ready! Let's eat!" Sal said.

Sal blessed the food and said a prayer. They all enjoyed dinner and each took turns telling the others about their day. Margo shared her grocery store experience with her husband and Curtis. The children passed around a sample of their flyer. The men recounted stories from work. Jonathon saw his opportunity and asked the reverend, "How come you never tell us about your job, Reverend Sal?"

"Well, mostly because I am supposed to keep my conversations confidential."

"Tell us about your life, then!" Katie requested.

"Oh, that's a *long* story because I am so *old!*" the reverend replied.

"Tell us anyway!" Jon pleaded. His parents gave him a reprimanding look. "I mean, you're not old. Please tell us."

"Well, I grew up in a small town in New Jersey. I was raised under a certain religion, and for the most part, I enjoyed going to church. I liked having the responsibility of being an altar boy. I felt so grown up when the priest would let me sip the wine! I liked the services because I loved hearing the stories of ancient times and of the miracles that Christ performed. But some things that were said would always leave a knot in my stomach. When I got older, I realized that those things were particular to that religion, and did not necessarily pertain to other Christian religions."

"We lived in a middle-class neighborhood, where there was always some ball game going on in the street after school. I liked to play, but I was never that good at it. I lived next door to a family of bullies. They knew that I never told on anyone, so they were always beating me up.

Sometimes they even stole money from me. My parents knew what was going on, but they never said anything. They didn't like to make waves in the neighborhood."

"My parents both worked very hard, and long hours, so I had to help around the house. That's how I learned to cook! I was pretty good at it, so I never had to clean. My parents made my brothers and sisters clean, while I cooked. We were poor compared to a lot of other people, and my brothers used to try to convince me that the meat my mother gave me to cook was actually roadkill. They were always trying to scare my sisters, too. If I made linguini, they told them it was tapeworms. When I hard-boiled eggs, they said they were eyeballs. You can imagine what they said about my spaghetti sauce!"

"Oh no!" Katie said.

"That's terrible," Jon added, looking at Katie.

"Oh, that's not even the half of it!" Sal added. "Since Mom made them do the wash, they would hang all of my underwear on the clothesline, and then invite all the neighborhood kids over to our yard for a game of badminton. One time, they put a saran wrap across my door in the middle of the night, and screamed '*fire!*' as loud as they could just to watch me bounce onto the floor! Then there were the usual buckets of water over the door, and tongue to the telephone pole tricks. Still wanna hear more?"

"No, Sal, I think they've heard quite enough for tonight," Margo interrupted. "You just officially became a *bad* influence on them! Giving them ideas!"

"Mom, we would never play those tricks on each other," Jon insisted.

"That's exactly what worries me! Who *would* you play those tricks on? Curtis, this is going to be a long four weeks with these two stuck in the house!"

"Well, they can actually be outside for next two weeks, even though they're contagious. The Herpes Zoster virus is present in the air in the spring from the lungs of all people who carry it. It is present outdoors naturally this time of year. It would be courteous of them not to cough, sneeze, or breathe intentionally on anyone, however."

"Great!" Sal said. "Then it's OK to go to the amusement park on Saturday?"

"Absolutely! As their doctor, I highly recommend it!" Curtis said.

Katie and Jonathon volunteered to clean up after dinner, and discussed what they had learned about Sal. He had given them the exact information that they needed to create a menu for tomorrow night's dinner!

The adults met in Sal's office to discuss plans for the flyer distribution, the creation of a newsletter, and the handling of the high volume of e-mails from the Web site. Sal volunteered to take all of the e-mails which were religious in nature, as well as any with negative intonations. Margo said that she had her hands full just handling the personal e-mails, but that she could create small groups for Curtis and Matt to handle, and wrote down responses to certain frequently asked questions. At this rate, they would each be responding to approximately a hundred to two hundred e-mails per day. They all agreed that if the hits continued to increase exponentially, they might even have to put Katie and Jonathon on e-mail duty.

Full from dinner and dessert, and exhausted from typing, the four friends said goodnight, and promised to meet at the church side door at 9:00 a.m. the next morning, to work on the broken-down house.

Chapter 12

Dinner Revenge

Katie, Margo, and Jonathon prepared sandwiches, snacks, and drinks for the men as they prepared themselves for the home improvement project. Curtis, Mike, and Matt helped Sal as he gathered tools and materials from the church basement. Once the van was loaded, Katie handed the men stacks of flyers, and they promised to do their best to distribute them without getting caught. It was illegal in most places to place flyers on cars in parking lots.

As the men drove away, Sal turned on the van radio, forgetting his promise to avoid media broadcasts. The news station was reporting that the Center for Disease Control (CDC) in Atlanta had confirmed the discovery of increased strands of DNA in certain people. Some were reported as having as many as twelve strands of DNA, versus the ordinary number of two strands, creating the well-known "double helix." Some people were volunteering to stay in Atlanta for observation. "Results are being sent in from all major hospitals around the nation. It is not yet known what caused these mutations, or what the ramifications will be. Some scientists are postulating that it was caused by exposure to some toxic substance, while others suspect that it is a natural evolutionary process. The public is being urged to not panic.

"In other news, ambassadors from all participating United Nations countries are being sent to the Middle East, in the hope of resolving recent conflicts."

Sal turned off the radio. The men all looked somber. He sensed their fear and confusion as well. "Does anyone here doubt that Planet Peace exists? Feel free to be honest," he asked.

"Well, as a matter of fact," Mike responded, "I'm not really sure."

"I can understand why you would feel that way. It's quite a stretch of the imagination," Sal answered. "But let me ask you all another question. Does anyone here doubt that there is God?"

All answered "No."

"That's excellent. When did you first realize or 'know' that there is God?"

"I knew it as soon as I laid eyes on my firstborn," Mike answered.

"I knew it when the Red Sox won the World Series. I'm originally from Chicago," Curtis confessed. "I never prayed so hard in my life!"

"And you're a healer! Surprising! No judgment," Sal assured him. "And you, Matt?"

"I knew that God existed ever since I can remember. I used to lie on my belly and watch ants and bugs in my backyard. There was such organization and coordination in their movement. It couldn't be by accident. I would watch nature shows on TV, and marvel at the systematic process of the food chain and the entire ecosystem. There's no way that such methodical systems could be randomly organized. When I was in college, I learned that the world's brightest mathematicians had concluded that it was statistically impossible for the human being to have evolved from a single-celled organism, unless it was organized by a highly intelligent force. That sounded like God to me!"

"But you didn't like going to church," Sal added.

"That's true. It left knots in my stomach, just like you mentioned at dinner last night. It wasn't until Margo introduced me to other forms of Christianity, that I relaxed into my faith."

"Well said. So we all believe in God. And we all know when we *knew* there was a God. We may not be sure how we feel about Planet Peace. But do we all realize the need, as human beings, as Earth citizens, or even as Christians, to increase in our faith, love, and charity?" Sal questioned.

"I was not raised as a Christian, but the older I get, the more I realize that I could increase in those skills," Curtis responded.

"I was raised as a Christian. Until recently, faith, hope, and charity were just words that I used to hear in church when I was a kid. Now that I see what's going on in the world, I realize that I don't want my kids to be raised in a world without those qualities. And it's going to have to begin with me," Mike answered.

"So, we have learned about the origin of our own personal faith, we realize that we don't want to live in a world without hope, and we are presently on our way to perform several acts of charity!" Sal exclaimed. "Lesson one completed: class dismissed!" he said as he parked the car in front of the Cawleys's house. Pat and Jan were still recovering, but both were expected to be released from the hospital by Monday morning. The men unloaded the car, and got to work on the Cawleys's house.

"Mom, can you take us to the grocery store?" Jon asked.

"Ugh, my favorite place! Why?" Margo asked.

"We're making dinner for everyone tonight," Katie answered.

"Do you have something in mind?"

"*Yes!*" both children answered at once.

"OK, you're making me nervous," Margo responded.

"Don't worry, I'm sure you'll enjoy every minute of it. I mean, every bite of it!" Katie assured her mother. Margo reluctantly agreed to take the kids to a store. She pulled on a scarf and glasses, and drove to a remote convenience market on the outside of town.

When the men returned, they found the table set for seven people. It was lit with candles, and had fresh flowers as a centerpiece. Because everything smelled so good, they were ready to begin eating, but Margo encouraged everyone to clean up first. As they arrived back into the shelter kitchen, they were greeted by Katie, serving "Les Yeux de Mer" on a silver tray lined with a doily. It was caviar-stuffed hard-boiled eggs.

"Oh, I get it," Matt said. "Eyes of the Sea. These are supposed to be eyeballs!" Katie nodded proudly.

Next came Jonathon, with a tray of cauliflower and cocktail sauce. "Now serving 'Cerveau Sanglant,'" he announced.

"We used to call this 'Blood and Brains' at our fraternity Halloween parties," Mike chuckled. Jon smiled, boldly.

Margo emerged from the kitchen into the dining area with a tray she called "Peau et Gluant." It contained large corn chips surrounding a small bowl of guacamole.

"Skin and Slime?" Sal asked.

"Yes, Reverend," she smiled.

"Bravo! It seems I have inspired some culinary genius in this family. You all continue to make me proud!"

Mike seemed confused as to why everyone was so impressed with tonight's menu. Matt explained why the children felt compelled to serve the reverend his *just desserts*.

After dining on "Roast Roadkill" (roast beef) and "Mystery Mash" (butternut squash), with a side of "Tapeworms and Toad Livers" (linguini and mushroom pasta salad), the meal was finished with a cup of "Worms and Dirt," made from ground Oreos layered in whipped cream and gummy worms.

"Touché, my friends. Tonight's dinner was *tres magnifique*!" Sal complemented the junior chefs.

"And how about you aiding and abetting these two," Matt said to Margo.

"Oh, I was barely an accomplice," Margo admitted. "The kids conjured up and cooked up the whole thing! I did warn them that it stops here, though. No buckets of water or yelling *'fire'* in the middle of the night!"

The men shared stories of the day's home improvement mishaps with Margo and the children. Sal joked that that's what happens when you put white-collar men into blue-collar shirts. But they all admitted that it felt good to leave the house in a better shape than when they found it, knowing that the elderly couple could return to a repaired home.

They told Katie and Jonathon that as they were placing flyers on cars in parking lots, people came up to them and took stacks of flyers from them to pass on to their families, friends, and coworkers. They were hungry for more information about the letter and the cubes.

"Speaking of hungry, anyone for more Worms and Dirt?" Curtis asked. Everyone groaned from either being full or disgusted. Margo handed Curtis the newly purchased garden shovel serving spoon and said, "Here, help yourself!"

Chapter 13

An Adventure-Filled Day

On Saturday morning, the Ellis family awoke to a Belgian waffle buffet. Sal escorted each family member through the buffet line, which was set up on the kitchen countertop. He helped everyone with their toppings and beverages.

"These waffles are huge!" Jon exclaimed.

"I'm guessing that you want us to be very full before we leave," Katie surmised.

"Well, park food can be very expensive," Sal responded, "and these cost only pennies to make."

"These are the best pennies I've ever eaten!" Matt said with a mouth full of food.

"How long of a ride is it to the amusement park?" Margo asked.

"Long enough for me to get started on lessons with Curtis," Sal answered. "It's Dorney Park, so we'll be a few hours."

"Yeah!" the kids shouted.

Sal made sure that everyone had their food, including Franklin, then joined the family with his own waffle. Each washed their own dish and utensils before heading off to shower and get dressed. Sal was already dressed and ready, so as he finished, he prepared snacks and drinks for the car ride. He printed out Katie and Jon's flyers for the parking lot, and sprayed each family member with sunblock, before loading the van.

"Sal, you think of everything," Margo mused.

"Well, you all are the closest things that I have to family here in Pennsylvania. I *have* to take care of you. And besides, you're my best tithers in church!" Sal joked.

"I doubt that." Margo laughed.

The Ellises piled into the van, and picked up Curtis at his home.

"Let's get out of here before Peterson spots us!" Curtis said, leaping into the van. "Thanks for saving me the copilot seat. I can get a little carsick when I sit in the back of a car too long."

"Oh, I had an ulterior motive," Sal responded. "Curtis, what's your definition of faith?" And so began Curtis's lessons with Sal.

Curtis decided that faith was a choice made by humans to believe in a higher power. Sal found that to be a very intellectual answer. He asked Curtis to tell him when he remembered feeling the most loved in all of his life. Curtis responded by telling the reverend about a memory from his childhood. He had fallen off a stone wall onto the asphalt driveway of his home and scraped both of his knees. His father found him crying and bleeding, and picked him up. The next thing Curtis knew, he was standing in the bathtub and his father was gently washing the blood and stones off his knees and legs. He dried and bandaged them, then he held Curtis to make sure that he was all right. They shared some of his grandmother's homemade chocolate cake, and his father made him laugh until he forgot all about his injured knees.

"Not only was that the moment that I felt the most loved, but I'm pretty sure it's when I decided to become a doctor as well. I was so moved by my father's caring, gentle spirit that I wanted to share that same feeling with others."

Sal said, "Curtis, I would like you to close your eyes and immerse yourself in that moment of caring. Feel the love that was being shared with you. Feel completely surrounded and filled with the love and caring." Sal watched as Curtis's face seemed younger and happier than he had ever recalled seeing it before.

"Now realize, Curtis, that God loves you a thousand times more than what you are feeling right now. So intensify the feeling. Try to magnify it ten times, one hundred times, or even one thousand times."

"Wow!" Curtis said. "My heart was racing and my adrenaline was pumping! How did you do that?"

"I didn't. You did! It's an exercise in increasing your love for God, and a meditation as well."

"Well, it worked! Not only on me, apparently," Curtis nodded his head toward the back of the van. The Ellis family had seized the opportunity to participate in one of Sal's guided meditations. They were all smiling faintly, eyes shut.

"Thank you, Reverend," Margo uttered. "That was a wonderful guided meditation. You are quite the multitasker! Driving and guiding us at the same time!"

"If you think *that's* something, you should see the batch of waffles he made while all that was going on!" Matt joked.

"Really?" Jonathon asked hopefully.

"No! Dad was just kidding," Katie answered.

"Aww!" Jon grumbled.

Everyone laughed and they all enjoyed the rest of the drive to Dorney Park. As he parked the van, Sal said "I hope you all like roller coasters!"

"Uh . . ." Matt said.

"Well, I uh . . ." Jon replied.

"Not me!" Katie added.

"We have roller coaster issues," Margo explained.

"I understand, family," Sal said reassuringly. "But we are actually here to increase our faith. When we face our fears, we realize that we are always safe in God's hands. So, allow me to guide you into 'my Father's house,'" and he motioned his hand toward the park entrance.

They passed through the turnstiles, and Sal handed in his passes. The six of them headed into the park.

"Let's start small," the reverend said. "This is a very simple roller coaster, designed in 1923. It was slightly revised in 1930. People have been safely riding these coasters for almost one hundred years. The worst thing about it is the noise." He guided the family and Curtis into the line for the "Thunderhawk." Curtis had no problem with roller coasters. The family reluctantly agreed to this coaster as a baby step. They each had had bad experiences on roller coasters in the past. But they trusted the reverend, and they wanted to increase their faith.

As the coaster started to ratchet uphill, the reverend said, "Remember when you felt the most loved . . ." They shut their eyes as the coaster pulled them higher. "Feel the love," Sal said, as it pulled higher. "Feel the caring," he continued, as it pulled them higher. "You are safe in his hands," the reverend said, as the coaster paused momentarily at the top. As it raced downhill and ratcheted around, each family member smiled and laughed and relished the feeling of flying through the air, and bouncing up and down, until they bumped to a stop. All at once, the Ellis family had cured their fear of roller coasters, and they proceeded to enjoy the rest of the day.

Each ride presented an opportunity for Sal to remind them that they are safe and protected. Even Curtis was glad for the reminders of faith, because he found that it took some of the edge off the pre-ride jitters. Ironically, Curtis had more of a fear of heights than of roller coasters. Twisting through space didn't scare him as much as being suspended at a high altitude. The Ferris wheel actually proved to be more challenging for Curtis than the "Talon," the "Hydra," or the "VooDoo." But Sal's reminders brought each one of them the comfort that they needed. Each one of them began to trust that even in the worst-case scenario, if they should fall to their death, their Creator would beckon them home, and they would be welcome in heaven.

The day flew by quickly, and soon it was time to head back home. Everyone grabbed a stack of flyers and stuck them to as many car windshields as possible. When they ran out of flyers, they all piled into the van and started home.

As they traveled down the PA Turnpike, they suddenly heard loud screeching noises. Sal shouted, "Pray with me! Thank you, Lord, our Creator, for keeping us safe in your hands," as he applied the van brakes, the tires squealed and dirt rose up in the air. He continued, "We trust Lord that you will protect this van and its occupants from harm, and we ask that you bless and keep safe all parties on this road. Amen." All responded, "Amen," just as the van came to a screaming halt, completely untouched by the shattered metal all around them. Sal, Curtis, and the Ellis family sat stunned, staring at the piles of wrecked vehicles all around them. One by one, they checked themselves over for cuts or bruises, but none had any. They each bowed their heads, and thanked God for their safety, then carefully stepped out of the van onto the road. Margo took Katie and Jonathon to the road shoulder, and advised them to stay there. Sal asked her to grab the first-aid kit out of the van and join him at the car in front of them. Curtis was ripping his shirt into strips to make tourniquets for a passenger in a nearby vehicle. Matt was helping some people to the side of the road, and covering them with a car blanket. Sal and Margo were helping people by cleaning and bandaging their cuts. Curtis shouted to the kids to dial 911 on their cell phones, then asked Margo and Sal to hold some passenger's heads still until the EMTs arrived. Smoke filled the air from people's airbags that had deployed. Curtis hadn't done this much triage since his first year in the ER. Matt was opening as many car doors as he could to let the smoke out, and to see who was in need of help. Thankfully, most of the people were unharmed, but in shock from the accident. He tried to get as many of them as possible to the side of the road in case one of the cars caught fire.

Soon, police cars and ambulances arrived at the scene. The police took statements from everyone, and the EMTs took a few of the drivers away on gurneys. Tow trucks were able to clear the area pretty quickly. There were enough vehicles there to transport everyone away from the scene in a matter of forty-five minutes. It was nothing short of miraculous. The six park-goers stood staring at each other when the last car was towed away, knowing that their prayers had been extremely impactful that day. All were profoundly changed by the day's events.

Chapter 14

A Surprising Sermon

"Good morning, Ladies and Gentlemen. I'd like to begin today's services by sharing with you something that happened to me and some friends yesterday," Reverend Sal shared with his congregation. He told them of the entire weekend, beginning with the repair of the Cawleys's home, the Dorney Park adventures, and finally, the accident. He explained how good it felt to commit the random acts of kindness for the elderly couple, and how proud he was to be able to reward his fellow workers with the gift of an amusement park ticket. He described the steps that he took to help some of them overcome their fears of roller coasters and other rides, and then revealed the story of the accident. It was cathartic for Sal to share this story with the congregation, and it left a lasting impression on each parishioner. His message was simple, but powerful: *thoughts and prayers have a direct impact on our world.*

He urged each of them to pray carefully and thoughtfully, with *expectation* about their own lives, but also encouraged them to pray with *expectation of peace,* when praying about world affairs. "You may feel as though your prayers could not possibly have an effect on world outcomes, but remember this law of physics: a particle acts not only like a particle, but also as a wave. And if we join together in prayer, our thought particles may create, or participate in, a bigger wave of peace."

After the service, the Ellis family approached Sal and congratulated him on his inspirational sermon. They told him that they felt ready to return to their home, and thanked him for his seemingly unending hospitality. Sal teared up at the idea of them leaving, but admitted that another parish family was about to lose their home to foreclosure, and that he would like to offer the shelter to them. They promised to continue their lessons with him weekly, and he promised to respond to e-mails nightly.

Curtis approached the group as they were making their way to the church reception room for refreshments. He introduced each one of them to his wife and two children. Curtis's family had stunned looks on their faces, as though they were meeting celebrities or heads of state. Curtis had shared with them that he was, and that the Ellises were, part of the group the reverend had spoken about.

"It's a great pleasure to meet all of you. When Curtis called yesterday, and told us about the accident, we all agreed to come home a day early to check on him," Yvonne Lasky explained. "We saw the news footage this morning from the helicopters that were overhead. It was absolutely amazing how your van was right in the middle of all of that wreckage, but completely unharmed!"

"It was just like the lava!" Curtis Lasky Jr. exclaimed.

"Like the lava?" Sal asked.

"He's talking about those fires in California last summer," Renee Lasky explained. Renee was the fourteen-year-old daughter of the Laskys'. "When the people had to evacuate from their houses, one person had called their home and left a long prayer on the answering machine. It was the only house that was untouched by the fire that came down the mountain. We saw it on the news."

"I see," the reverend said. "Makes you really appreciate the power of prayer, doesn't it?" Curtis Lasky Jr. nodded his head. "Let's get some refreshments."

The Ellis family packed up their things and headed home. It had only been a week, but it seemed like an eternity since they had fled their home. They felt sentimental about their church now. It would never be just a place to visit on Sundays any longer. From now on, they would always think of it as a haven of safety, and a school, and as the place where they bonded with Sal. He met them at the door as they finished packing up Matt's truck.

"So, you're really leaving, huh?" Sal asked.

"It's time, Reverend," Margo answered. "Besides, you have a new family to minister to."

"And *feed*!" Jon added.

"Yes, yes, new people to feed, Jon. Will you be jealous? Maybe I'll have to check in on you over the next few weeks, and see how the pox are coming along."

"OK, but no funny business, Reverend."

"No funny business! You wouldn't recognize me if I wasn't funny, would you?"

"That's true, Reverend," Katie said. "We'll miss you. Please come visit us often."

"You bet, Katie. Now get out of here, all of you. I've got work to do. Menus to plan, and all of that," he said, shaking hands with Jon and Matt, and hugging Katie and Margo. "See you online tonight!" he added.

Curtis was pleasantly surprised that his family cared so much about his well-being that they cut their visit short to come home to him. He was completely blindsided when Yvonne asked if they could stay with him. It had been one year since they had signed the divorce papers and the three had moved out.

"Stay? Of course, but . . ."

"Listen Curtis, this thing really shook up the kids. And me. The idea that we might have lost you, well, it was too much to bear. I'm not saying that it won't be difficult or that we won't have problems but, well, maybe I was too hasty in calling for a divorce."

Curtis was floored and elated at the same time. He was still reeling from the trauma and the drama of the previous day's events, and now he suddenly felt like he must be in the middle of the best dream he ever had.

"It will be great to have you all back. I mean it. And listen, I'll really try to hear everything that you say, and be there for you, and . . ."

"Curtis, don't try so hard," Yvonne interrupted. "I've done a lot of thinking and I'm pretty sure that *I* was the one who wasn't listening, or being there for *you*. Let's go home."

Phil Peterson was pulling weeds in his flowerbed when the Laskys arrived home.

"Uh-oh, don't give him too much information. He doesn't like the Ellis family," Curtis warned his family.

"Well, look who's here! Coming for a visit, kids?" Peterson asked.

"Something like that," Yvonne answered nervously.

"You missed my barbecue yesterday, Curtis," Phil said.

"Yeah, sorry about that, Phil. Something came up."

"Well, if you're looking for a Memorial Day picnic, you won't have to look far. Those nuts who've been picketing and protesting the fence around those damn boxes are planning a big celebration tomorrow. They have a big sign on the property that says 'Memorial Day Picnic Monday.'" I called the cops, but they said since the property is temporarily unavailable for our use, we might as well let them have their fun. Can you believe that nonsense? Why do *they* need to have fun? And on *my* property!"

"I don't know, Phil. Well, we're gonna head inside now and have some lunch. Say 'hello' to Mary for us!" Curtis said.

"Will do. Nice to see you, Evette."

"*Yvonne!*" the kids shouted in unison.

"Whatever," Peterson muttered.

Chapter 15

Plans and Preparations

The Ellis family was glad to be home, and each one of them heaved a big sigh of relief as they walked through their front door and set their belongings down. Franklin immediately began barking and running from room to room. This was his way of inviting a game of chase, which the children were happy to indulge in. Matt checked the phone messages while Margo started the laundry. After unpacking the suitcases and ordering take-out food, they decided to check their e-mails. Each day seemed to bring at least one hundred new hits to the Planet Peace site. People seemed compelled to read Rebecca's letter, to share it with others, and wanted to talk about it. Margo and Matt were happy to oblige. Matt answered as many e-mails as he could before it was time to pick up the Chinese food. Margo decided to stay and check in on the chat room. "Cubecutie" was informing everyone that she was organizing a Memorial Day picnic on the Petersons's property, and she was inviting all who attended the chat room to come along. Margo asked her if she needed any help, and she told Margo that everyone was to bring something. "Cubecutie" would be arriving at the site by seven in the morning, and she welcomed anyone who would be willing to join her to set up tables and chairs, and to start the grill. Margo inquired if she thought they might be asked to leave by the police or other authorities, but "Cutie" insisted that she had surreptitiously found out that they would be left alone.

Sal signed into the chat room as "Radical Rev," asking "Cutie" if she needed any help on the grill. "Cubecutie" responded that that would be great. Margo asked the reverend if he would speak to the group, and he agreed that it would be a good idea. They decided that he should also say grace at the picnic. People in the chat room were asking if they could bring guests who had not logged onto the Planet Peace Web site, and Margo and Sal agreed that all would be welcome.

"Curtis, come quickly!" Yvonne urged. "It's Phil Peterson!" She thrust the phone at him.

"Phil? What's happening?" Curtis asked.

"It's Mary! I can't wake her up!" Peterson cried.

"I'll be right over," Curtis slammed down the phone.

Curtis found Mary asleep on top of the bedcovers. Every effort that he made to wake her was to no avail. He even ran home to get some smelling salts, but nothing woke her. They dialed 911 to request an ambulance. Curtis found that Mary had taken a very common pain reliever, but it was a new bottle, and most of the pills were still inside.

"She takes that stuff like candy," Phil complained. "We buy huge bottles of it at our warehouse club, and she goes through it like it's going out of style."

"The problem with these over-the-counter pain medicines is that people believe that they can take that many without doing any harm to their bodies," Curtis told Phil. "This one has a warning that says that you should not exceed 1,000 doses in one lifetime." He pointed to the bottle label.

"What can happen if you take 1,000 doses?"

"It can cause vital organs to shut down and can lead to a coma."

"Oh my god! Is that what happened to Mary?"

"It's possible, Phil. But let's not be hasty. We'll let the doctors at the hospital determine what's going on with Mary. Come on, I'll follow the ambulance. I'll stay until you need a ride home."

"I sure appreciate everything you're doing, Curtis."

"That's what neighbors are for, Phil."

Curtis's suspicions about Mary's condition proved to be true. She had lapsed into a coma from taking a common pain reliever. Phil became so distraught that he began to have chest pain. He grew pale and sweaty, and it quickly became apparent that he was in cardiac arrest. Phil had phoned his daughter on Curtis's cell phone on the way to the hospital, and she was going to stop at her parents' home to get her mother's insurance information before joining them at the hospital. Curtis realized that he had better warn her that both of her parents were now receiving medical treatment.

"Thank you, Dr. Lasky, I appreciate your call," Lila Peterson said.

"It's no trouble, Lila. I'll see you in the emergency room in a few minutes," Curtis said.

Curtis phoned Yvonne to ask her if she would please call Margo to let her know that he would not be available to help out with the Web site this evening. Yvonne agreed, but decided to check out the Web site before calling. She was decidedly impressed by Rebecca's letter, and by the intensity of Margo's testimonial. She phoned Margo to deliver her former husband's message.

"Thanks for the heads-up, Yvonne. Did you say that Petersons's daughter's name was 'Lila?'"

"Yes. Why?"

"I went to high school with a 'Lila Peterson.' In fact, she became Miss Pennsylvania. She was quite a big deal. Heard she's had a failed marriage or two since then. Do you know if she's still living in California?"

"It's my understanding that she is currently living with her parents. Shall I tell Curtis to give her a message for you?"

"No, no, that's OK. She probably doesn't even know I'm alive. I mean, we weren't exactly friends or anything. I just hope her folks are OK."

"Me, too. That's awful to have both of them ill like that. By the way, Margo, I really enjoyed looking over your Web site. I understand that there's a Memorial Day picnic being held on that property tomorrow. Will you be there?"

"Yes I will. And how did you hear about that?"

"Phil told us when we got home from church. He had seen a sign posted there. He said that he called the police and tried to stop it, but they said to just let everyone have their fun."

"Yeah, I heard that we're going to be left alone. Anyway, at this point, who would be around to press charges?"

"Ooh, that's right. Well, I thought we'd bring the kids down. Will yours be there, too?"

"Yes! The more, the merrier! Just bring a dish or two."

"OK, I'll do that. I'm so curious to take a closer look at those cubes!"

"They're really fascinating. It'll be great to see you, Yvonne. And thanks for calling." The two signed off and began preparing for the picnic.

Lila Peterson arrived at the emergency room and found that her mother had already been taken to have a CAT scan. Curtis greeted her at the reception window, and brought her to where her father was being treated. Phil Peterson's color was now a grayish shade of blue, and he was vomiting.

"Dad!" Lila shouted as she ran to his side.

"Lila, I'm not doing too well. Take care of your mother," Peterson instructed his daughter, as he lost consciousness. Curtis started shouting codes and messages, and EMTs who were waiting by the door came running with paddles to administer a shock to Phil's heart. Another doctor started shouting orders, and a flurry of nurses and aides came running to administer last-minute lifesaving measures. But Lila's arrival was not a minute too soon. She turned to Curtis and started sobbing into his chest. The hospital staff offered their condolences, as they dejectedly removed all of the reviving apparatus.

Curtis was a comfort to his neighbor, Lila, although he felt completely helpless and inadequate. He brought her to the patient grieving room, which was empty, thankfully. He poured her a cup of tea, which she had no intention of drinking. Her hands were shaking so violently that she couldn't even hold the cup, but she set it on a corner table and warmed her hands around it.

"Thank you, Dr. Lasky, for all that you've done today. I don't know what I would have done if you weren't here. I'm sorry that my father was not a better neighbor to you over the years."

"First of all, it's time you started calling me 'Curtis,' and second, I can name plenty of times when your dad came through for me."

"But I've called you 'Dr. Lasky' all of my life! I don't think I can stop now."

"Well, that makes me feel old. But it just shows what a great job your parents did with you: raising you with good manners."

Lila and Curtis made some small talk until she was ready to check on her mother, who had been admitted to the Intensive Care Unit.

"I'm sorry for the loss of your father, Ms. Peterson," Mary's doctor offered, "but I can't lie to you. It doesn't look good for your mom. There is very minimal brain activity. I recommend that you start making preparations." Lila found herself leaning on her neighbor once more. She had recently moved back home from California, and her childhood friends had all moved to different states. She was literally alone, having just received her second set of divorce papers a week earlier.

Curtis had excused himself for a moment to phone Yvonne. "Hey, babe, things are not good here. Phil has passed away, and Mary isn't doing well. I know that tonight was supposed to kick off our new beginning as a family, but is there a chance . . ."

"Of course, she can come over, Curtis. You don't have to ask. Lila is absolutely welcome to come here. She can even stay over if she doesn't want to be alone. I'll make up the spare bedroom. And I'll keep some dinner warm for both of you."

"Thanks. You're a doll," Curtis signed off with his ex-wife, as he marveled at her spirit of generosity. The old Yvonne would have been insanely jealous of her husband spending the entire day with a former beauty queen. Yvonne grew tired of women throwing themselves at her husband. She never trusted him to remain faithful to her, although he would never succumb to infidelity. She smiled to herself, as she made the bed and prepared some dinner. It occurred to her that she had increased in the qualities of faith, love, and altruism all at once.

Chapter 16

Memorial Day Picnic

"Cubecutie's" name was Alice Brown, and she and Margo shook hands, introduced themselves, and began setting up for the picnic.

"I brought every chair that I could find," Alice said.

"So did I," Margo replied, hopeful that every seat would be filled, and more.

Matt had phoned Curtis and asked him to help him set up some tables. Curtis and his children arrived with their own tables. Renee and Curtis Lasky Jr. eagerly set up tablecloths and covered dishes sent along by their mother. Mike and Candy came along with more patio chairs, and Jodi pulled up with a trunk full of snack trays and food. Just as everyone was about to head back home to pick up more food, Sal pulled up in the church van with a volleyball net, and various other pieces of athletic equipment. After setting up the net, the adults discussed what the proper actions should be regarding Phil Peterson's passing, and Mary's condition.

"Is Lila OK with us being here today?" Margo asked Curtis.

"Yes. In fact she plans on stopping by for a few minutes. She wants to talk to you."

"Really?" Margo seemed surprised.

"I'll be sure to pray for the Peterson family during grace, and I'll be sure to mention that we keep them in our prayers during our talk today," Sal said.

"Thanks, Reverend. Maybe I'll have the kids make up a little flyer, and we can even take up an offering for Lila," Margo said.

"Lila doesn't look like she's hurting for money, but I suppose she could always donate it to the charity of her choice," Curtis offered.

The picnic turnout was much greater than anyone had expected. Thankfully, most people brought lawn chairs, and enough supplies to feed their own families. Everyone mingled and took the time to examine the cubes firsthand, and undisturbed by authorities. Katie and Jonathon passed out some flyers regarding the Peterson family, and collected donations for Lila. Sal brought the group to order with a prayer for the Petersons, the Ellis family, and for world peace. He concluded his prayer by mentioning that he was organizing a class called "The Three Qualities," and that he would be hosting weekly prayer and meditation groups on Saturday evenings, with their focus on world peace.

Mike approached Curtis about Sal's classes. He was intrigued by Rebecca's letter, by the cubes, and by the huge turnout at the picnic. Candy was not as convinced, and they were not members of Sal's church, but Mike figured if Curtis was willing to take the classes, then he would be willing to join him. Curtis confided that he was thinking of joining the group and told Mike that he would be happy to carpool on Saturday evenings. Yvonne joined the men and told them of her interest in joining Sal's classes. They all agreed and told Sal the news. The reverend was delighted and surprised them by telling them that he had already enrolled Barbara, Mike's sister, as his first student.

Lila managed to pull herself together enough to drive to her parents' new property for the picnic. She spotted Margo, and approached her as she was cleaning up some of the food refuse.

"Hi, Margo. I don't know if you remember me. I'm Lila Peterson."

"Lila, hi, oh, I was so sorry to hear about your father. How's your mom?"

"Not so good. Thanks for asking. Listen, Margo, I just wanted to let you know that I don't have any problem with whatever you want to do on this property. I saw you on the news that day and I knew that you were telling the truth. I could just feel it."

"Thanks, Lila. I don't know what to say,"

"You don't have to say anything. I went on your Planet Peace Web site and read Rebecca's letter. It was absolutely alluring! I couldn't stop reading it."

"I know what you mean."

"So I just want you to know that I'm going to try to get these goons off your back, and see if I can get them to just leave this property alone."

"I really appreciate that, Lila, but you've got your hands full right now,"

"No, listen, it's no bother," Lila interrupted. "I'm not working right now, and, in fact I'm taking some time off to figure out my life's direction, so don't even give it a second thought."

Margo thanked Lila again, and introduced her to Sal and the others. She graciously thanked each one of them for their condolences, and for their charitable donations. She told them that she was thinking of making a donation to the hospital, so their timing was perfect. Lila enjoyed listening to Sal speak. Amid the divorce, her father's loss, and her mother's illness, she was desperately in need of some spiritual guidance. Sal suggested that she might consider joining "The Three Qualities" class and the weekly prayer and meditation group. Lila thought that that might just cure both her loneliness and her spiritual misdirection. She agreed to be at Saturday's first meeting.

When Candy learned that both her husband, and his sister Barbara were joining Sal's classes, she felt a little bit left out. As much as she loved Margo and Matt, she just didn't know what to make of this cube thing and its letter. She asked Margo's friend Jodi what she thought about all of this.

"Honestly, Candy, I'm not sure what to think of all of this, either. I mean, Margo is my dearest friend, and I value her opinions. I trust her level of sanity, and obviously a lot of other people do as well," Jodi said, referring to the large gathering of people. "But this planet in the future thing seems so 'out there,'"

"Yeah, *literally*!" Candy said. They both laughed. "I've decided to help Margo to deliver flyers to show my support of her, personally."

"I told her that I want to come along the next time they volunteer at the soup kitchen, also," Jodi added.

"Well, at least she knows who her friends are."

"*That's* for sure," Jodi answered.

"What's for sure?" Yvonne asked, joining the two. Yvonne knew Candy from the school PTA meetings, and was introduced to Jodi earlier in the day.

"It's for sure that Margo and Matt know who their friends are," Jodi answered.

"I agree. It's absolutely evident. And look at how many friends they didn't even know that they had! The sign-up sheets for flyer distribution and for Sal's classes are already full! With all of that exposure, they're going to need help answering e-mails. I told Margo that I would be happy to help. Curtis answers about one hundred e-mails a night for her."

"Really?" Candy and Jodi asked in unison.

"Yes. You should consider helping her, too. She's going to have her hands full, once all of those flyers go out!"

Candy and Jodi looked at each other in amazement. This Web site was only one week old, and Curtis was already answering one hundred e-mails a night? The women knew that the Ellises each answered one hundred e-mails each night themselves. It occurred to them that these cubes and their accompanying letter were nothing short of a phenomenon.

Chapter 17

Lending a Hand

Lila was at the funeral home, making arrangements for her father, when she received a call from the hospital. Her mother's vital signs were declining, and she was urged to come quickly. She phoned Yvonne to let her know, and Yvonne offered to drive her to the hospital. Lila decided that it would be a good idea. Yvonne picked Lila up at the funeral home, and the two left for the hospital.

Matt had talked Margo into visiting the nursing home with him on this day. He had an extra day off due to the holiday, and he found himself missing his parents. Margo agreed to join him, as long as he agreed to put some time into the soup kitchen with her.

"Both in one day?" he asked.

"Sure! Why not?" she asked.

"OK, but I think that will be my charity quota for the whole week," Matt joked.

The couple enjoyed their day with Matt's parents and their friends at the nursing home. They drove into the city, had an early lunch, and then volunteered to serve lunch at the soup kitchen. Margo introduced Matt to all of the people that she had previously met there. Each of them told her that they had found the Planet Peace Web site, and that they were joining in on the chat room almost every night. They had told most of their relatives and friends about it, too, many of whom were also in the chat room each night. They asked how Katie and Jonathon were doing, and Margo confided that they had been purposely infected with chicken pox, so she didn't bring them. The volunteers were intrigued by the idea that chicken pox could strengthen the immune system, and some of them asked the Ellises if they could expose their own children to them to see if they could contract the disease. Margo told them that she would be happy to host a "pox party," and promised to give them a call when the pox popped out. After serving lunch to hundreds of people, Matt and Margo spent several hours cleaning up. When they realized that it was time to head home, they decided to pick up some dinner instead of cooking that night.

When they arrived home, Matt and Margo discovered that their children were covered in spots. Katie was prepared, so as soon as they started itching, she started applying the calamine lotion with cotton balls, and she and Jonathon were wearing their oven mitts.

"I'm very proud of you for handling this, Katie," Margo said.

"Why didn't you call us?" Matt asked.

"It's no big deal, Dad," she answered. "It's not rocket science."

"Speaking of rocket science," Jon joined in," these solar eclipse fanatics called and wanted to know if they could have a party on the Petersons's property in August!"

"What?" Margo and Matt asked simultaneously.

"They want to know if they can have their solar eclipse party on the Petersons's property in August, when the next full solar eclipse takes place. I took the guy's phone number and told him that you'd call him back."

Jonathon's parents sat staring at him, and then at each other for a few seconds, before anyone spoke.

"We thought you'd be happy," Katie said.

"Why would you think that?" Margo asked.

"Because these people understand solar eclipses, and we need one to understand the cubes better," Katie answered.

"That *does* seem logical," Matt said, hesitating, "but do we really know who these people are? And how did they get our phone number?"

"They got the flyer, and they've been in the chat room," Jon answered.

"They saw you on TV, Mom, and two of their kids go to our school, so they got our number from the school directory," Katie said.

"Oh," Margo said. She seemed relieved that there was a reasonable trail of events. "Well, your father is right. We need to make sure that these people are just enthusiastic stargazers and not creepy stalkers who want to vandalize the Petersons's property."

"Relax, Mom," Katie assured her mother, "we know this family, and they're harmless. The kids are total brainiacs, and their parents are total hippies."

"Oh," Matt and Margo sighed together.

"So, how are you two feeling?" Margo asked. She proceeded to take care of the family, while Matt doled out everyone's share of bucket chicken and sides.

"Wait," Jon said, "does Sal know what we're having for dinner tonight?" They all laughed, and Jon's parents assured him that Sal had nothing to do with tonight's dinner.

Lila was able to hold her mother's hand until she passed. She wasn't sure how well she did with her promise to her father of taking care of her mother. But she felt that it was best that they make their transition together. The more she thought about it, the more at peace she felt. Her father would have wanted to be the first to die, so that he could lead her mother into the next world. Phil was a leader, and Mary was a follower. And Lila was now completely alone. She was just starting to get used to the new divorce, and now she had to cope with being without parents. Thankfully, she had great neighbors in the Laskys and a new circle of friends. The thought of a new life with them made her feel unusually optimistic.

Yvonne invited Lila to stay over again that night, and she accepted. They both agreed that she could pick up her car at the funeral home tomorrow. Curtis greeted them at the door with his condolences. When he received Yvonne's call from the hospital, he decided to leave work early and to make dinner. He allowed the children to eat in the family room, so that the three of them could talk in the kitchen. Lila thanked them both for their hospitality and for their friendship. She promised to pay them back some day. They assured her that it was not necessary, but she insisted that they would be repaid.

"I've learned how powerful words are," Lila said. "Without your word, you are nothing. And I am a woman of my word." She excused herself and went to bed early. She cried herself to sleep, knowing deep down that everything would eventually be all right.

Curtis and Yvonne began answering their share of e-mails. They communicated (via the chat room) to the Ellises that Mary Peterson had passed. The Ellises expressed their regret, and told the Laskys that the pox had arrived.

"I don't know whether to say 'sorry' or 'you're welcome!'" Curtis responded.

"We *are* grateful, Curtis. We'll get through this, don't worry," Margo replied.

"I'll check in on the kids on my way home from work tomorrow," Curtis promised.

"Me, too!" joined "Radical Rev."

"The kids will be glad to see both of you," Matt typed. He also told them about the family that wanted to have a solar eclipse party on the Petersons's property. He had arranged a lunch date with them for Friday, to find out what they had in mind for the party. Matt promised to let them know what he learned from that meeting.

Margo indicated that it might be a good idea to have these people there at the time of the solar eclipse, since they are knowledgeable about astronomy. She mentioned that they were very impressed with Rebecca's letter.

Both Sal and Curtis seemed relieved that this new family had an appreciation for the Planet Peace Web site, and that they were not just another set of curious onlookers. They agreed that it might be helpful to have them there to decipher the clear cube message in August. Curtis assured everyone that Lila would be agreeable to the late summer gathering. The friends all signed off, promising to check on each other the next day.

Chapter 18

Serendipitous Meetings

Margo called Candy and Jodi and asked them to go to a "Big Sister" meeting later that evening. She had asked Yvonne the night before, but Yvonne felt the need to be around for Lila and for her children. She hadn't spent much time with them since moving back in with their father, and she wanted to make sure that they were adjusting well to the change.

Candy and Jodi both agreed to go to the meeting, as long as the three could go out for coffee afterward. They discussed the Memorial Day picnic, and shared stories of the people that they met, and the conversations that they had. All agreed that everyone that they had met were extremely nice ordinary people, with an intense curiosity regarding the cubes and Planet Peace. They rehashed how well the day had proceeded, from the preparation, to the barbecue, to the prayers, and athletic events. Candy revealed that they had raised over $500 for Lila's donation. Jodi remarked that Sal had twenty people signed up for his class, which he considered to be full and closed. Margo shared that fifty people had signed up for flyer delivery.

"There certainly was a spirit of volunteerism," Margo said.

"Well, I think that stemmed from the altruism or charity suggested by Rebecca's letter, don't you?" Jodi asked.

"I'm not sure," Margo answered. "But I know that after tonight's meeting, I'm sure that I have room in my life to help one more little girl."

Margo's friends agreed that they, too, had room in their lives to help out the "Big Sister" organization.

Yvonne accompanied Lila to the funeral home to resume preparations for her father's funeral, and to add to those a service for her mother as well. A double viewing was arranged for Thursday evening, and the funeral and burial for Friday morning. Lila thanked the funeral home director for his time and for allowing her to leave her car overnight. He assured her that everything regarding the services for her parents would go smoothly. Yvonne and Lila left with their cars and decided to grab a quick lunch to eat in the nearby park. They both decided that some fresh air would do them good.

True to their word, both Sal and Curtis arrived at the Ellises' home after work to check on the newly speckled children. Curtis commended Katie on the expert care that she was administering to herself and to her brother. Sal commended both children on their efforts regarding the Planet Peace flyer production, as well as their help at the Memorial Day picnic. The kids modestly accepted the praise, admitting that they had nothing better to do, as they didn't have school or homework for almost two weeks.

"Then this package must have arrived not a moment too soon," Margo exclaimed, speaking about a box that had come in the mail from the school principal. "Mrs. Demberg has forwarded your schoolwork through the end of the year!"

"Ugh," Jonathon sighed.

"What a doll!" Katie added sarcastically.

Margo doled out the various packets of work to the children, and then asked them how they felt about the prospect of having a "pox party."

"Who would come?" Jon asked.

"Well, we could keep it small, and just invite our volunteer friends from the soup kitchen, or we could have a bigger party by inviting all of our new friends that we met at the picnic."

"In all fairness to the kids, they probably shouldn't be overstimulated with a large party like that because they still need their rest at this point," Curtis interrupted.

"That's true," Margo said. "Well, what about a small gathering?"

"I guess it would be OK with me," Katie answered.

"Me, too," Jon agreed.

"OK, then, I'll go make some phone calls."

Margo spent the following day helping the children with their homework and preparing for the "pox" gathering. She also stopped at the dry cleaners to pick up some suits that Matt had dropped off. He had anticipated that they might need their best suits cleaned for the funeral tomorrow. When she returned from the dry cleaners, Margo saw a florist truck pulling up behind her. She ran into the house to set the suits down and turned back to the door to receive two enormous bouquets. They were addressed to Katie and Jonathon.

"Kids, somebody has sent you a gift!" Margo shouted. Katie and Jon came running in their pajamas to the door.

"Who are they from?" Katie asked.

"Who would send *me* flowers?" Jon asked.

"They're from Sal!" Katie exclaimed. The children read their cards.

"In honor of my friends who are dotted,

Please enjoy these orchids spotted" Jon read.

"As your body heals with glorious powers,

Please enjoy these spotted flowers!" Katie read. "They're beautiful! He is really too much!"

"Oh, yeah, he's too much, all right," Jon answered, "but too much of what?"

Matt was amused by the flowers and the cards that accompanied them. He had arrived home from work early that evening in order to help Margo to get ready for the soup kitchen volunteers. He also reminded Margo that they had a lunch appointment with the solar eclipse enthusiasts.

"What were their names, again?" she asked.

"Ruth and Karl Leonard," Matt answered.

"Oh, yeah. And where are we meeting them?"

"At the Green Collar Café. I told them that we'd be there by one o'clock."

"Perfect. That will give us plenty of time to get there from the funeral, and plenty of time to get home and be ready for our guests."

The meeting with the Leonards went well. They were pleasant and ordinary-looking people who had a great respect for nature and for astronomy. They knew the owners of the Green Collar Café, and the Ellises found them very easy to talk with. They had seen the broadcast of Margo's testimonial, and they had read Rebecca's letter on the Planet Peace Web site. They were disappointed that they had missed the Memorial Day picnic at the cube site because they had made prior arrangements.

Margo filled them in on all the happenings behind the scenes of the cube incident, including the radiation inspection and the turmoil with the Petersons. She also shared some of the details about Sal and the Dorney Park trip. The Leonards sounded interested in meeting the reverend, and thought they might bring their children to his service on Sunday. The Ellises thanked Ruth and Karl for agreeing to meet them and told them to call or e-mail if they had any questions, or whenever they wanted to begin planning the "solar eclipse" party. Margo agreed to post a link to Ruth's Web site to obtain volunteers for the late-summer gathering.

Chapter 19

Open-Mindedness

The soup-kitchen volunteers were pleased to gather at the Ellises' home on Friday evening. The party was low-key, as everyone had had an exhausting week. The adults chatted amiably, as the children played video games. The party began wrapping up around 9:00 p.m. It had been a full couple of days for Margo and her neighbors, following the viewing and the funeral of the Petersons. Each event had a larger turnout than expected, due to the exposure given at the Memorial Day picnic. Additional collections had been compiled to be added into Lila Peterson's final donation to the hospital that had cared for her parents.

This was the first topic of discussion at Sal's first class on Saturday evening. He was quick to commend all who had contributed monetarily to Lila Peterson's cause and used those contributions to segue into the altruism aspect of his "Three Qualities" class. The reverend had prepared worksheets for the class with questions that he had asked the Ellises during their first lessons with him. He asked everyone to journal their answers and promised to meet with them on an individual basis at the end of every class. Each member of the class was to sign up for their private time slot on a sheet that was passed around the room.

Sal's questionnaire had a ring of familiarity for Curtis who had already experienced his first lesson with Sal a week earlier, during the Dorney Park trip.

The questionnaire asked its reader their opinion of Rebecca's letter, and if they had any doubt that Planet Peace exists. It also asked them to define faith, and to record the time that they felt the most loved in their lives. It also asked that they state their immediate plans to help their fellow man.

Sal's lessons were often Bible classes, mixed with life lessons, and woven into the "faith, love, and altruism" theme. Occasionally, he would mix in a quote from a different religious text, emphasizing the similarity between religions. It was easy for Sal to find examples of the "three qualities" within all types of spiritual works and publications, as it was a common thread throughout the history of mankind.

Sal was a fan of the Bible Code mystery. The Bible Code is a mathematical equation that can be applied to any text, but it has remarkable findings when applied to the Old Testament of the Bible. When one applies the equation and seeks out historical events, details of the events appear on the same page. For example, when one applies the equation and seeks out the name of a particular person in history who has been assassinated, one will find the date of the assassination, the city, and potentially, the assassin's name as well as other details. Sal had learned that the world's greatest mathematicians and statisticians had thoroughly inspected the code, and found it to be indisputably impeccable. Those who discovered the Bible code warned, however, that certain Bible "predictions" have not come true, and estimate that intervention of human thoughts and interactions intercepted those events from happening. Sal related the opinions of the discoverers of the Bible Code to his class:

"The founders of these equations, and the authors of the books about these equations, believe that mankind has unlocked a code that was *meant* to be unlocked by humans with the help of computers some day. They also believed that once man laid eyes on these predictions, they could make choices and decisions that could change history. That is actually one of the reasons that we are here in this class: to change history.

"You believe that you are here to increase in your level of faith in God, love of God, and kindness toward your fellow man, correct?" Everyone nodded.

"If just one of you increases in any one of those, will it change the course of history?" All answered, "Yes."

"If *all* of you increase in all three categories, will it change the course of history?" All answered, "Yes," again.

"St. Thomas said that every thought is a prayer. Do you agree with him?"

All nodded in agreement.

"So if we pray together, do you believe that we can change the course of history?" Sal's students smiled brightly and assentingly. "Then what shall we pray for?"

"World peace," was the universal response from the class.

"What is this, a 'Miss America Pageant?'" Sal joked. "No, seriously, I am in agreement with you. I believe that human thoughts are forms of energy, and when we combine our thoughts in unison, we can make a difference. Science has documented this in double-blind studies of people who had heart disease. Certain patients were prayed for, and others were not. The ones who were prayed for healed better than those who did not.

"We live in a world where most people believe that it will come to an end. Our prayers will be up against all of those thoughts, but if we can hold tight to a vision of something greater for humanity, we may be able to make some kind of difference. And will it be worth a try?" The students responded with yes, and absolutely!

"Great!" Sal said. "Let's get started."

Over the next few months, Sal's month-long classes remained full, and the prayer and meditation group which followed the class grew increasingly larger. Candy and Jodi ended up joining the class, as well as other neighbors and friends, and each of Sal's Sunday morning services left standing-room-only crowds hungry for more. The Planet Peace Web site grew such a large audience, that Sal's students were all asked to answer some of the e-mails. Katie and Jonathon recovered easily from the chicken pox, and finished their schoolwork ahead of schedule. They teamed up with the Leonard's children in planning the Solar Eclipse party. The summer flew by, and Sal kept things lively by taking large groups of his students bungee jumping and hang gliding. He used these activities to help his students to increase in their faith and to trust in a higher power to keep them safe. Although Margo had greatly increased in her level of faith, she nearly fainted when Sal brought a tarantula to class one evening and encouraged everyone to pet it.

Everything seemed to be going well for Sal, for the Planet Peace Web site, and for the "solar eclipse" party. But the Washington DC scientists and the NASA officials who had visited the cube site were still in a conundrum about what to do with the site. A representative of each group called Lila consistently, urging her to build privacy walls around the property, or to have it condemned. In July, Lila found herself face-to-face with the DC representative, when he rang the doorbell, interrupting her sun-tanning repose in the backyard. He was just as surprised to see a beautiful bikini-clad model come to the door, as she was to see a scientist.

"Pardon me, ma'am, is this the residence of a Lila Peterson?"

"That's me, how can I help you?"

"I'm Dr. Steven Morano with the Department of Environmental Protection. I'm the one who has been calling you these last several weeks."

"You mean, you're *one* of the people who have been calling me for the last several weeks," Lila corrected.

"Yes, well, do mind if I come in?"

"Actually, I'm kind of busy right now."

"This will only take a minute. I just have some research that I'd like you to take a look at and some papers that I need you to sign."

Lila did her best to fend off the visitor, but eventually she let him in and allowed him to present his case. He told her that she needed to fear for her health on the cube property and tried to prove that it was a liability to own such a toxic piece of land. She told him that she was not afraid, and that she had no intentions of signing anything without legal representation. He left copies of his documentation with her, and saw himself to the door. As Lila was closing the door, he surprised her again with an invitation to dinner. She surprised herself by answering "yes."

As Steven Morano was boarding his return flight from Philadelphia International Airport to Reagan International, David Kaiser's plane was landing in Philly from Florida. Kaiser was NASA's unidentified stationary object specialist. He had flown up to Pennsylvania before when NASA was first notified of the presence of the cubes. He had performed the preliminary testing of the property, the cubes, and the letter, and he was present when the Ellises, the Petersons, and the first responders were all checked for radiation. He was determined to get Lila Peterson to take some action on the cube property that would both protect the public and get his superiors off his back.

Lila was on her way out to a photo shoot, when David pulled up in a BMW rental.

"Listen, can you move that thing? I'm going to be late!" she yelled.

"Are you, Lila Peterson?"

"Yes"

"David Kaiser, NASA Special Officer," he showed her his identification.

"Oh no, not again. Look, I'm gonna be late. I've got to be in Philly by ten o'clock."

"Hop in, I'll drive you. It'll give us a chance to get acquainted."

"Not interested. Besides, it will just make me your captive audience for all of your ridiculous reasons for wanting me to abandon my parents' property."

"Oh, my condolences, by the way. I was awfully sorry to hear of their passing."

"Thank you. Now can you please get out of the way?"

"What can I do to convince you to get in? Buy you lunch? Treat you to some Philadelphia culture after your appointment? A Philly cheese steak? The Liberty Bell?"

Just then, Lila realized that she had no gasoline in her car and no money in her wallet. She knew that if they did not leave right then, that she would be late for her shoot, and her agent would never forgive her. She reluctantly climbed into the passenger seat, and they headed toward the city.

Chapter 20

Thoughts of the Future

With the "total solar eclipse" party just weeks away, everyone was busy making preparations. Katie and Jonathon were, of course, making and distributing flyers. The Leonard and Lasky children were all eager to help. Margo, her neighbors, and all of Sal's students were fielding e-mails all day, each day. Margo feared that the property would not be large enough to accommodate the size of the expected crowd. She commissioned some pretzel vendors and Port-O-Potty facilities for the event. Ruth and Karl Leonard were rallying all of their stargazing friends, and Alice Brown ("Cubecutie") volunteered to organize the Planet Peace attendees.

Lila Peterson had her hands full with the two scientists who had coincidentally both become her new suitors. Somehow, she had managed to keep their attention away from the property. She was fairly certain that neither one of them knew anything about the solar eclipse party. It felt good for Lila to be in front of the bright lights and wind machines of the modeling studios. She was grateful to have reconciled with her former agent in Philadelphia. All of this new activity was instrumental in distracting her from the loss of her parents, but at the same time, it facilitated her ability to cope with their loss in her down times.

She still enjoyed attending Sal's Wednesday evening classes, and Saturday meditation groups. Several members of the group had organized regular trips into the city to read books to children in the pediatric wings of the major hospitals. Some of them had also become members of the Literacy Mentor's group, and others had signed up to build a home for Habitat for Humanity. Lila was particularly interested in a mission's trip that one fellow classmate was organizing, but she was afraid that it would never come to pass for her if she were to be successful in teleporting to Planet Peace.

Lila would catch herself having a thought such as the teleportation and immediately question her own sanity. *How could one entertain an idea like this?* Yet something inside her would assure her that this phenomenon was a *real* possibility. She was determined, at the very least, to give it a try. And if she found herself stuck here on Earth for the rest of her days, then she would simply find ways to make the best of it. While the war in the Middle East was ramping up daily, the United States had managed to stay fairly neutral. News broadcasters mentioned the word "miracle" to describe U.S. neutrality nightly. Politicians, ambassadors, and statesmen of all kinds also used the word "miraculous" to describe the U.S.'s unfailing neutrality stance. Sal's group felt some ownership and responsibility for helping to keep their country out of the war with their intense prayers and peace meditations. Lila wasn't sure how effective her prayers were, but she was fond of the classes nonetheless.

Margo was also questioning her sanity frequently. The practical side of her was able to complete her daily tasks as though life would go on this way forever. From grocery shopping, to doing laundry, to housecleaning, and minding her accounts that she still managed from home, Margo was still able to keep one foot on the ground. But with each passing day, she had to wonder if she would be doing these things for much longer. She found herself daydreaming about what Planet Peace must be like, and her dreams were becoming more and more vivid.

Matt immersed himself deeply into his work to try to avoid having thoughts of Planet Peace. But it was always on his way home from work that he would allow his thoughts to wander there. He found himself worried that a member of his family might be left behind, or that Franklin might not be able to make it. He decided to take up this fear with Sal, and see if he could come up with any sage advice.

Sal brought the subject up in Saturday night's meditation class, and opened it up for discussion.

"Some of you have been expressing some concerns as the time draws near for our celestial experiment. We have become experts at facing our fears, and more importantly, at remembering God in times of fear, to dispel the anxiety, and trust in the right outcome for all parties concerned. So, some of the questions that I have been approached with are: What if one or more of my family members is unable to teleport? What if my pets are unable to teleport? What will become of my earthly possessions? I suggest that we bow our heads and pray for guidance on this issue, and follow the prayer with discussion."

The group did as they were instructed. When the prayer was through, they began talking amongst themselves about caring for each other's children and pets, and assisting any loved ones that might be left behind with any worldly possessions.

"My kids will have a fit if they have to move back out to Seattle with relatives. They like it much better on this side of the country," Yvonne told Lila.

"I would be more than happy to take care of them if I should be left behind, Yvonne." Lila said.

"I couldn't impose such a tremendous burden on you like that, and in the prime of your life!"

"I would consider it a great honor to take care of your wonderful children. But your relatives might protest unless I am made their guardian in your absence. Maybe we should get this in writing."

"That's a great idea. We need to revise our wills anyway. My hope is that the children will be able to come with us, of course."

"If the three of us do not make it on a first try, and, by chance, you and Curtis do make it, I promise that I will give every effort to get them to you in any subsequent trials."

"Lila, I can't tell you how much comfort this brings me," Yvonne said, welling up with tears. "You would really do all of this for us?"

"Yvonne, I can't believe that you would even ask me that, in light of all that you've done for me in the last few months." Lila's cell phone buzzed with a text message. "It's David Kaiser, the NASA guy from Florida. He wants me to move down there and live with him."

"Sounds serious," Yvonne was actually wondering out loud, rather than making a statement.

"It's not, really. Actually, both he and Steven—that's the Washington DC guy—want me to consider moving in with them. Neither one knows about the other. I like them both, but let's face it: I have more in common with the people in this class than I have with those guys!"

Yvonne told Curtis about her conversation with Lila on the way home from class. She told him of Lila's offer to take care of their children.

"Mike and Candy also agreed to look after our kids, but I got the feeling that Candy was still a bit hesitant. I wouldn't be a bit surprised if she did not even give the cubes a try," Curtis said.

"No doubt. She's been a skeptic from the start. I'm not sure if it's her love for Margo or sheer curiosity that has gotten her this far."

"Well, only time will tell if those things will actually work. I have to say that I have no regrets. I love the people that we have met, Sal's classes, and how I have grown as a person. I may feel a little foolish if the cubes don't take us anywhere, but at least we can all feel foolish together. And I can't think of a nicer group of people to feel foolish together with!"

"Me, too," Yvonne laughed.

Chapter 21

This is It!

The weeks prior to the "solar eclipse" party seemed to move in slow motion. All of the attendees had one thing on their minds as they proceeded through their daily tasks. It was one surreal moment after another, and each one of them was experiencing emotions and sensations ranging from excitement and hyperactivity, to exhaustion and hypomobility. Some were even prone to anxiety attacks. Little by little, the details of the party fell together, and as the day approached, a calm came over everyone. The Ellis family arrived on the Peterson property to find a local folk-singing band setting up. As they tuned their instruments, Margo felt assured that, at the very least, it would be a great party, and people would be amused.

Alice Brown greeted the Ellises with glasses of her homemade lemonade, and Ruth and Karl Leonard greeted them with big smiles and warm hugs. They began to set up chairs and tables, as they had done months earlier for the Memorial Day picnic. People began arriving with lawn chairs and blankets. Some brought covered dishes, and others brought bags of chips, pretzels, and popcorn. Friends reunited in the afternoon sun's rays, and new friends were introduced until everyone felt comfortable in their immediate surroundings.

Sal addressed the crowd: "Hello everyone, and welcome to our solar eclipse extravaganza!" Sal quipped. "We are very fortunate to be here in each other's company on this warm summer day, under a beautiful blue sky. We find ourselves in the company of old friends and new friends, and yet it feels like a family reunion of people that we've known all of our lives." Everyone nodded and smiled in agreement. "Today's festivities were organized largely by Ruth and Karl Leonard, with the help of Margo Ellis," Sal barely finished saying the names before the crowd clapped and cheered wildly. "We owe each of them a debt of gratitude," Sal was interrupted with cheering again. "They have asked me to say an opening prayer, which I more than happy to do. But before we begin, I must acknowledge these people for their bravery, their courage, their knowledge, and their efforts," Sal was barely able to finish his sentences before the roaring crowd. "Please, let me finish. None of us knows how this event will turn out. As humans, we are all well aware of the feeling of triumph and of disappointment, and I imagine that we have all imagined this event turning out both ways. What would be the best-case scenario? That by virtue of today's forecasted solar eclipse, we will somehow be able to unlock the code to these mysterious cubes. Even better: that we might be able to utilize what we learn, in order to live out the rest of our lives in a place of nirvana, albeit ecstasy." The crowd began to rise in cheering, but Sal quieted them with a motion of his hands. "The worst-case scenario? That, in the company of friends, old and new, we enjoy a pleasant afternoon and evening together, observing a natural celestial event, remain ignorant as to the usefulness of these boxes, but make the best of the evening with culinary delights and musical entertainment," Sal motioned toward the musicians, causing the audience to clap and cheer again. "Either way, it sounds like a good time may be had by all," Sal allowed the cheering to settle down. "So let us pray," Sal continued, "as we bow our heads, we humbly gather in your name, Lord, our Creator. We realize that all goodness comes from you, and that life's mysteries are too great for us to solve. The bounty of this Earth and all of its miracles has been beyond our comprehension as a human race. We come before you, Lord, in prayer, asking that you enlighten us as to our purpose and our destiny, making the way abundantly clear. We pray that you keep safe each person and pet that is here today, and along any of their subsequent journeys. We commit to keeping thoughts of you at the center of all of our actions. We commit to faith in you, love for you, and to goodwill toward our fellow man, woman, and child. We thank you for protection, clarity, and fruitfulness. In the name of the Creator of all, we pray." The crowd answered, "Amen," then the cheering resumed.

The afternoon progressed with people helping themselves to hamburgers and hot dogs on the grill, and sides at the tables. The band played, as spectators mingled and introduced themselves and their families to other families. It felt like any other ordinary late-summer picnic. A warm breeze permeated the air, carrying the smells of summer and a promise of fall. Dragonflies swarmed, and crickets began warming up for the evening. Margo's heart leaped when she saw the first firefly of the day, because it reminded her that they were there to witness something in the dark. She grabbed Matt's hand for comfort, and he reassuringly put his arm around her. They gathered the kids to their lawn chairs, and sat together as a family in front of the cubes, as though they were about to watch a fireworks display.

The heavens did not disappoint the crowd. The eclipse began to take place very slowly, and even though it was still daytime, Sal began to light the citronella torches for light. People had brought camping lanterns and flashlights as well. Karl Leonard went up to the podium and began to address the gathering.

"In ancient times, people feared the loss of the sun's light during a solar eclipse. Eastern civilizations used to believe that there was a dragon that was eating the sun, and they would bang loud objects together to try and chase the dragon away. Some even immersed themselves in bodies of water in order to pay homage to the Sun so that it was better able to fight off the dragon. Solar eclipses were also thought of as bad omens in ancient times. In *Paradise Lost*, Milton described the wariness of Europeans:

> As when the sun, new risen,
> Looks through the horizontal misty air,
> Shorn of his beams, or from behind the Moon,
> In dim eclipse, disastrous twilight sheds
> On half the nations and with fear of change
> Perplexes Monarchs.

"Even as late in history as the time of Christopher Columbus, people feared the loss of the sun's light. A tale is told that while in Jamaica, Columbus and his crew were denied certain supplies. In an effort to get the native Jamaicans to comply with his wishes, Columbus threatened to take the sun from the sky. Knowledgeable as he was about astronomy, the sun vanished due to a solar eclipse. The natives were all too pleased to supply Columbus and all of his crew ample sustenance and supplies for their journey, when the sun happily returned to the sky.

"Later in history, Mark Twain would use the same scenario with his main character in *A Connecticut Yankee in King Arthur's Court*. His character, Hank Morgan, threatens to remove the sun from the sky if he is not freed from the stake that he is about to be burned at. His captors are happy to free him as the shadow of the Earth finishes its journey across the sun's light. Modern science has made all of the awe and terror and superstition of days gone by seem uncivilized, as we chart and foretell celestial events, and they transpire just as they are predicted. Nonetheless, it does not take away from their beauty, and their rare occurrence. For these reasons alone, people gather to observe and to share their experiences, as they would any other light show. But tonight, perhaps something special will occur. Perhaps, something extra . . ."

As Karl spoke, the Earth's shadow on the moon was crossing in front of the sun, obliterating the light. Streaks of red light could be seen all around the edge of the dark orb, and for a brief moment, the clear cube, inscribed with its cryptic messages and drawings, was alit with luminescent writings. Cameras began flashing, taking pictures of the spectacle, as breaths were drawn in everywhere. The gasping of air, along with the flashing and clicking of cameras, was all that could be heard, as words escaped everyone present, and no eye blinked for fear of missing a single second of this mysterious moment.

Margo's mouth was open, and her right hand was over her heart. She could feel it pounding so hard that it was almost as though she was literally touching it. Aside from being astounded at what she had just witnessed, she was grateful that she was sitting down, because she felt sure that she would have fallen otherwise. Matt had jumped up to try to bring others back to their lawn chairs. When people saw the luminescent writing, they wanted to get closer to it, but Matt realized that they might get in the way of the photography. The solar eclipse enthusiasts were accustomed to photographing these events, and they were prepared with their cameras, tripods, and appropriate film for documenting the words which appeared on the clear cube. The children had all stayed seated with their parents, clutching their pets. The folk singers and their band members were conferring as to whether or not to play. Karl Leonard spoke again, as the sparks of red gave way to fuller sunbeams, "And here comes the sun," he said.

The band immediately broke into the familiar Beatles tune by the same name. A mixture of nervous laughter and low-level cheering and whistling blended into their musical introduction.

Modern photographic equipment produced images almost immediately. The photographers set the images through enlarging devices, and beautiful photographs of the spectacle appeared immediately. Onlookers could not help but "ooh" and "ah" at the illustrations of a spectacular experience that had happened just moments earlier. Further enlargements allowed them to read clearly the instructions for generating the power to mobilize the contents of the cube. It seemed as though the cubes themselves would remain, as the contents would be transported or teleported into another dimension.

The instructions called for portable generators, various types of fuel, and machinery. The primary components, however, seemed to be large quantities of gems and metals, which caused some of the attendees to become suspicious. Mutterings about this event being the subject of an elaborate jewel heist permeated the crowd. The Leonards were quick to assemble the photographic material, and Karl returned quickly to the podium. "Well, it appears that we got what we came here for! How about that beautiful performance by Mother Nature?!" Karl was trying to steer the crowd into some applause and positive thinking. It worked, as the mob exploded into thunderous applause. He motioned Sal to the podium, and turned the microphone over to him.

Sal settled the group with his hand, then asked for one more round of applause for the musicians, to which the throng was more than happy to oblige. Sal decided it would be best if he wrapped up the presentations for the day, and allow the evening to progress as naturally as possible. "Let us give thanks to our Creator for the beautiful spectacle of light and darkness that we were permitted to witness," the people bowed their heads and prayed. "Lord. We cannot begin to express our gratitude for the wondrous and awe-inspiring sights on this planet and in the heavens. There is no shortage of things to ponder and to marvel at in this world. We who are assembled here are blessed by good health, happiness, and prosperity, and we are surrounded by love. Keeping in mind that you are the source of all good things, we pray for your continued blessings and guidance."

The crowd responded with an "Amen." "We will take all of the time that we need to process the information that we have received, and our astronomy experts will analyze and interpret the data for our edification and understanding. As always, we will be in full communication with each other via our chat rooms, our Web sites and our classes. I suggest that we turn any and all of our anxieties and suspicions over to prayer, and that we lean on each other for continued support. Now let us enjoy the food that was lovingly prepared for today, and the company of good friends and family."

The gathering of people did exactly as they were told by Sal. They joked and laughed and enjoyed each other's company. A small group of the solar eclipse enthusiasts, led by Karl Leonard, gathered up their equipment and their findings and proceeded home to their computers for analysis.

It would take only weeks before all the materials required for teleportation were assembled. But the instructions stated explicitly that the vehicle was not to be tested until 2018. The next scheduled meeting of the "Solar Eclipse Enthusiasts" was set for New Year's Eve, 2017.

Edwards Brothers,Inc!
Thorofare, NJ 08086
12 August, 2010
BA2010224